THE PROSPECT
OF DETACHMENT

Michael Denneny, General Editor

Stonewall Inn Editions

Buddies by Ethan Mordden
Joseph and the Old Man by Christopher Davis
Blackbird by Larry Duplechan
Gay Priest by Malcolm Boyd
Privates by Gene Horowitz
Taking Care of Mrs. Carroll by Paul Monette
Conversations with My Elders by Boze Hadleigh
Epidemic of Courage by Lon Nungesser
One Last Waltz by Ethan Mordden
Gay Spirit by Mark Thompson
As If After Sex by Joseph Torchia
The Mayor of Castro Street by Randy Shilts
Nocturnes for the King of Naples by Edmund White
Alienated Affections by Seymour Kleinberg
Sunday's Child by Edward Phillips
The God of Ecstasy by Arthur Evans
Valley of the Shadow by Christopher Davis
Love Alone by Paul Monette
The Boys and Their Baby by Larry Wolff
On Being Gay by Brian McNaught
Parisian Lives by Samuel M. Steward
Living the Spirit by Will Roscoe, ed.
Everybody Loves You by Ethan Mordden
Untold Decades by Robert Patrick
Gay and Lesbian Poetry in Our Time by Carl Morse and Joan Larkin, eds.
Reports from the holocaust: the making of an AIDS activist by Larry Kramer
Personal Dispatches by John Preston, ed.
Tangled Up in Blue by Larry Duplechan
How to Go to the Movies by Quentin Crisp
Just Say No by Larry Kramer
The Prospect of Detachment by Lindsley Cameron

Stonewall Inn Mysteries

Death Takes the Stage by Donald Ward
Sherlock Holmes and the Mysterious Friend of Oscar Wilde by Russell A.
  Brown
A Simple Suburban Murder by Mark Richard Zubro

THE PROSPECT OF DETACHMENT

LINDSLEY CAMERON

ST. MARTIN'S PRESS • NEW YORK

Library of Congress Cataloging-in-Publication Data

Cameron, Lindsley.
    The prospect of detachment / Lindsley Cameron.
        p.   cm.
    ISBN 0-312-05496-3
    I. Title.
    PS3553.A4338P7   1988
    813'.54—dc19   88-17673

First Paperback Edition
10 9 8 7 6 5 4 3 2 1

C O N T E N T S

THE PROSPECT
OF DETACHMENT

FOR MARCEL, OSCAR,
AND THE SHADE
OF NATSUME SOSEKI

The moment Scott and Harvey left the apartment, I began screeching. "Oscar! They're going to castrate us tomorrow!" I was horrified to hear myself say it. It made it seem all the more real. I found I couldn't stop looking at my balls, just to make sure they were still there.

"What does that mean?" Oscar is my cousin, and sometimes my lover, although that seems like an awfully active word to apply to someone as barely extant as Oscar. (He's magnificent to look at, but he has a learning disability. Harvey and Scott say it's due to overbreeding. Being such a near relative, I find the implication rather insulting. Besides, it is distressing to hear one's servants—the descendants of peasants!—speak so disrespectfully of an ancient Persian family.)

I explained. Oscar rolled over on his back, splaying his hind legs as if to surrender his scrotum to the knife.

"Marcel," he drawled in that maddening way he has, "nothing is going to happen tomorrow. It never does."

I couldn't control the furious twitching of my tail. "Oscar," I wailed, "this is an emergency! How can I make you realize? It's going to happen—and it's going to happen *tomorrow*—unless we do something. This isn't one of those projects they talk about and never get around to, like refinishing the floor. They've been talking about it for weeks, but I only just figured out what they meant. How was I to know? They kept saying 'fixed' as if we were broken appliances or something. As if sexuality were a crossed wire."

"Well," Oscar said, rolling over on his side to get a closer look at a dust ball under the couch, "maybe it is." Then he stared at this dust ball with a kind of disgusted amazement, the way Harvey looks when he shuts the bedroom door on me and lies down on his back—which is how he always memorizes his lines—and I slink through the transom and leap soundlessly to the floor and creep under the bed and sneak over the end and voilà! there I am, sitting on his face.

It was an utterly unremarkable dust ball. It hadn't done anything ingenious. Oscar is always bestowing his attention—such as it is—on unworthy objects.

"They take good care of us," he purred unconcernedly. "If that's what they want to do to us, it's probably for the best."

Oscar has no imagination. His attitude was all the more exasperating in that he himself had brought on this threat. They would never have noticed we were maturing if it hadn't been for Oscar's little indiscretion with Mrs. Lovett. (Oscar doesn't have any particular sexual orientation. In fact, there are times when I think the concept of gender is beyond his grasp.)

Mrs. Lovett lives upstairs. Her servant is a tiresome

man called Duane. I find both of them very vulgar. It would be difficult to say which of the two I dislike more.

No one in our household likes Duane.

"You have to feel sorry for him," Scott often says after one of Duane's visits. (Duane is a great one for dropping in.)

"No you don't," Harvey tells him. But once he added, "The trouble is, you get to feeling guilty for *not* feeling sorry for him."

It will really be Duane's fault if we're emasculated, because no one would have known Mrs. Lovett was in heat if Duane hadn't started making coy remarks about it. He's always bringing Mrs. Lovett down here—to "play" with us, as he so disgustingly says. He has a shrill, nasal voice, not unlike Mrs. Lovett's. "Keep those boys downstairs! I don't want a litter on my hands," he simpered.

That was the trouble, it was the way he put it. Of course, *because* Duane told them about Mrs. Lovett's disgusting condition, Harvey and Scott thought it was the mating instinct that led Oscar out the kitchen window and up the fire escape and into Mrs. Lovett's window. But that's nonsense. The call of the wild is remarkably weak in Oscar, primitive though he is.

He's suggestible. And awfully dim. He only catches one word in every ten he hears. When Duane made his little speech about Mrs. Lovett, all that registered with Oscar was "stairs" and "litter." So later on, when he found himself on the wrong side of a locked bathroom door, Oscar, in a rare burst of thought, came to the conclusion that the litter box must have been taken upstairs.

And before I realized he was gone, he had managed not only to find his way out of our kitchen and into Mrs. Lovett's but also, in the course of entering her window, to knock over two quiches that were cooling on the sill and a cachepot (after Boucher) containing a flowerpot full of growing basil. As these things shattered, they spread themselves all over the kitchen—Oscar remembers noticing pieces of piecrust on the ceiling—in a way I would have found very satisfying.

Destruction is my art form. I have spent my life perfecting it, and I don't think it's immodest to say that I have pulled off some pretty impressive effects in my time, considering the limited means of expression I have at my disposal.

But Oscar is no artist. I must admit, he's pulled off some pretty impressive effects in his time, too, but he deserves no credit for them. They were all accidental, including this one.

And poor Oscar can never enjoy his own performance pieces because loud noises terrify him. Actually, most things terrify him. That's why I can't help thinking that Mrs. Lovett must have behaved in a remarkably forward manner on this occasion, because when things are shattering and crashing, it is Oscar's way to run as far as he can from the noise and hide under a lot of soft things in some dark place—he favors Harvey's closet for this purpose—until he forgets what he's hiding from.

On the other hand, he may have thought of Mrs. Lovett as a hiding place. (He has no notion of his size: He's always trying to hide behind things that are smaller than he is.) Be that as it may, the fact is that Duane discovered him copulating with Mrs. Lovett in the middle of the kitchen floor, surrounded by clumps of potting earth, shards of porcelain and terra cotta, and soggy fragments of asparagus quiche. Love among the ruins.

Duane pulled him roughly away from Mrs. Lovett. Oscar inflicted what damage he could while Duane was searching for his keys. The results were really very pleasing. Considering how abruptly the opportunity arose, and the traumatized state he was in, I think he managed very well.

What he achieved was a kind of cartooning by accentuation. The gash on Duane's nose was as broad and as deep as a claw could gouge it. And as the skin around it reddened and swelled—as it had already begun doing by the time Duane showed up at our door, holding Oscar at arm's length in a grubby WNCN canvas tote bag with the top bunched together in his trembling hand—Duane's nose, which is excessively large to begin with, was at least twice its normal size. And the deformation of this protuberance somehow portrayed Duane's soul, captured his essence. So I think it would have to be called a successful caricature.

Of course, it cannot be compared with the craftsman-ship of my major attack on Duane a few weeks ago, but then I had had the advantage of being able to plan carefully in advance. Duane was going out on what he vulgarly re-ferred to as a "hot date." (Duane has no lover, which is unsurprising considering his total lack of charm.) He had been popping in on Harvey and Scott almost daily to show them each item he acquired for the occasion, so that I knew exactly what to go for when the night arrived and he stood displaying himself in his Parachute pants, rotating fatu-ously like something on a spit.

I had schemed for days, working out how to inflict the maximum damage with the minimum exertion, for I think economy is essential to High Art. Nothing superfluous.

There is a corner bracket next to the entrance to our living room, and on this bracket rests a spiky contemporary sculpture that I have never found congenial. I could never bring myself to knock it over, though, because making it teeter back and forth is so amusing, and really, I have so little to amuse me when Scott and Harvey aren't home.

I practiced diligently. I found that by bounding up to the bracket at the sound of the front door opening, I could conceal myself behind this sculpture by the time whoever came in the door reached the entrance of our living room.

An artist must explore all the possibilities of his media. I had discovered that I could induce diarrhea by eating Scott's sunblock. It tastes frightful, but an artist must make sacrifices. And my pains were well repaid, I must say.

But an artist must also be prepared to improvise. As I crouched, waiting for Duane to move into my springing range, I realized that if I aimed the sculpture at Duane's head as I leapt, Scott and Harvey would be occupied in saving it rather than defending Duane.

My flexibility in this matter was also rewarded. The falling sculpture not only diverted my servants, but wrought much pleasing havoc as its spikes entangled themselves in Duane's hair and snagged his shirt in several places. Truly, Duane's ensemble could not have been more amenable to destruction if it had been chosen expressly for my gratification.

Although action—and speedy action at that—was obviously called for, Oscar and I wasted most of the day in bickering reminiscence about these incidents. I have often noticed Scott and Harvey behaving in a similar way when the rent is due.

Oscar actually suggested that if my performance that night had been less successful, Duane would not have been so insistent that Scott and Harvey should get us fixed. "I know I did the right thing," I told him. "To worry about consequences is to compromise one's art."

Oscar is a most unsatisfactory conversationalist. He doesn't understand a tenth of what's said to him. He did not appreciate my point at all. All that he said was, "I wonder what's for dinner."

"Who cares?" I snapped. "I defy *anyone* to tell me the difference between the Elite Entrée and the Fancy Feast." For that is what our dinners are labeled. That's the world for you. One pretty name after another for the same ugly realities.

I gave myself over to gloomy reflections. What a cruel irony, I thought, if I should be desexed now, when the only lover I have ever known is Oscar. Why, that's as bad as having no experience at all. Worse, possibly.

I watched Oscar for a while. He had developed a fleeting interest in a small cockroach. Oscar's fur is a beautifully subtle color, the palest strawberry blond, and ethereally fluffy. As he watched the bug scuttling along the floorboards, his eyes brightened and his expression became almost intelligent. I thought of making love to him, just in case I never got another chance. But it was no use, I was too disgusted with him. And I suppose I was too frightened.

I could feel myself beginning to give way under the terrible pressure of the situation. Desperate for inspiration, I turned to the catnip mouse that is suspended from a rail under one of the chairs in the kitchen. That catnip mouse is insidious. One thinks there can be no harm in a whiff or two to calm one down, but taking a whiff or two has a way of altering one's judgment so that taking many whiffs comes to seem like an irresistibly inviting course of action, and before one can analyze what's happening, one is conspicuously stoned. As though from far away, one can hear the laughter of Harvey and Scott. It is humiliating to be laughed at by one's servants, but somehow whenever I start sniffing at the catnip mouse, I forget what the consequences will be.

By the time Scott and Harvey came home that evening, I was positively unhinged. As though to underline the inevitability of our impending doom, they gave us real fish for dinner. They only do that when they're feeling guilty about something they're going to do to us. It was whiting, which I thought said something very disappointing about the extent of their guilt. The last time they gave us real fish, it was swordfish. That was the night before they left for a whole week, leaving us to be fed and brushed by Duane, who never emptied our litter box.

I had no heart to eat the whiting. Oscar ate both our portions. His imperviousness made me feel even worse. Lonely. And progressively desperate.

I paced back and forth through the apartment in conspicuous agitation. "It's almost as though he knew," Harvey said.

Of course I could not sleep. Mechanically, I investigated every door and window in the apartment, but of course they were all locked. I knew they would be.

Sometime around dawn I padded into the bedroom.

Harvey and Scott were lying back to back, as far from one another as the width of the mattress would allow. There's an image of gratified passion for you. I looked at my servants for a long time, meditating on the vanity of sexual relationships. For a moment I had thoughts of resigning myself, succumbing to the operation with good grace.

But then I fell to brooding bitterly about Oscar again. It occurred to me that my disillusionment was unworthy of me. What was it based on, after all? Experience with one retarded cousin forced on me by circumstances beyond my control. I'll be damned if I'm going to spend the rest of my life with nothing sexual to remember but him, I thought.

It occurred to me that I might yet induce Scott and Harvey to spare me. In a gentle bound, I attained a bottom corner of the mattress. I decided to address myself to Harvey. I'm not sure whether he is the more compassionate of the two, but he's the one I have always found more amenable to manipulation. I crept up to his groin and began licking his balls. My action was intended as a statement. I thought it would bring home to him what he was causing me to loose.

He smiled. This was all very well, but I realized that I had accomplished only half of my purpose. I may have reminded Harvey that testicles are nice things to have, a source of many pleasing sensations, but I was delivering this message too subliminally. Harvey, being asleep, would be unlikely to connect this thought with Me. I opened my jaws and bit.

I thought I was being quite subtle. It was nothing but a gentle little nip, really, yet the next thing I knew Harvey, roaring obscenely, had flung me right across the room.

He was sitting up in bed staring at his groin with an expression of horrified surprise. That was not what I had intended. I had hoped to induce a mood of gentle erotic melancholy.

But it was obviously too late for that. Temporizing, I turned my face down to lick my right foreleg in a pitiful way while I composed my features in an expression of betrayed innocence. I hoped that my manner would suggest that I had leapt in to defend Harvey's private parts from an attack by some vicious stinging insect, only to have my loyal vigilance repaid by this outrage on my person.

It took some time before I could get his attention. His roaring and thrashing about had wakened Scott, who of course required an explanation of the rumpus. And by the time he had made Scott understand, I realized that I was really hurt. My right foreleg hung flaccidly in front of me. I could not move it at all. The pain was excruciating.

Remembering the whiting, I doubted Harvey would really care about what he'd done to me, but I kept mewing as wretchedly as I could. What with the mounting pain and my mounting panic, as Scott and then Harvey investigated my injury, my memory of the morning's events is unclear.

By the time I heard the vet say, ". . . postpone the operation until his leg is healed," and Harvey say, "Then I guess we'll wait and have Oscar taken care of at the same time," I thought it was something I was imagining in delirium. But it must have been true, because here I am, as virile as ever, stumping around the apartment in a cast and getting sashimi for dinner every night. Of course, the threat is still hanging over us, but now I have plenty of time to plan how to avert it.

Oscar, of course, doesn't appreciate what I went through to win this reprieve for us. "I told you it wouldn't happen," is all he says.

HELL ON WHEELS

FOR JOHN MERCER

It is a truth acknowledged by un-married women in Manhattan that a single man in possession of a large disposable income must be gay. Therefore, when Mr. Palmer joined the staff of Blenheim Associates (as Junior Creative Director), their only female employee to find his arrival interesting was Mrs. Wilberforce, the fag hag. At lunch hours, young men surrounded her like chorus boys backing up a fading star. Mr. Palmer fitted in very well with that crowd, and it never crossed anyone's mind that he might be straight.

One night, however, Mr. Palmer, who had lingered in her apartment gossiping about the other, departed guests, embraced her in a manner she had assumed he reserved for his own sex. For Mr. Palmer was in fact a straight man, of sorts. His tastes were rarefied: He was attracted only to fag hags. (No slang term exists, as yet, for his predilection. It is, of course, one way for a man to enjoy the company of gay men without acknowledging his motivation.)

Mrs. Wilberforce was astonished. She put it to herself afterward that, having had no means of anticipating his advances, she had had no time to make up her mind to reject them.

Fear soon succeeded surprise as their relations continued. For it was Mrs. Wilberforce's misfortune to work for Kiki Kroesig (Vice President, Creative Communications), a manager so violently opposed to office affairs that she had warned Mrs. Wilberforce, "If I ever hear of your carrying on with anyone at Blenheim, you're fired." Mrs. Wilberforce did not enjoy working for Ms. Kroesig, but, as what Blenheim called a "displaced homemaker," she had discovered that a woman of forty who has never worked is in no position to be choosy about employers. Indeed, she swiftly realized that Blenheim had merely taken her on as cannon fodder for Ms. Kroesig, who lost her assistants (whether through her tantrums or their despair) at the approximate rate of one every five weeks. Retaining her position for over a year, Mrs. Wilberforce was already a fixture, and her popularity among the gay segment of Blenheim's staff derived in some part from her unremitting victimization by the notoriously homophobic Ms. K.

Mrs. Wilberforce confided her apprehensions for her livelihood to Mr. Palmer.

"Oh," he told her airily, "I think you're safe. I haven't said anything."

"I didn't mean I thought you would. But don't you think people may suspect?"

"In the first place, who would?" he countered. "And in the second place, even if they did, no one would tell Kiki. Who would talk to her if they could help it?"

Mrs. Wilberforce found this reassurance inadequate. "Everyone knows my job is hell on wheels, but there are people around here who would do anything for a chance to write copy, believe it or not. They even toady to *me*. It's pathetic."

"Listen, sweetheart, as far as everyone around here is

concerned, I'm one of the boys, and if I wasn't, you wouldn't give me the time of day."

She looked unconvinced.

"The positioning strategy has been an unqualified success in the target market," he insisted.

"You *always* underestimate consumers' sophistication," she complained. (It was an argument they had often had in meetings of the Creative Department.) "You're talking about people who've spent the past six months selling 'the hip potato chip,' 'the battery that never dies,' and 'film that's finally foolproof.' "

"You're proving my point," he told her. "You knew it when you wrote those slogans. Would you try to sell 'film that costs twice as much as the competitors', but might be a little bit easier to use, depending on your camera'? Given the choice between a truth like that and a nice, catchy lie like 'finally foolproof,' people will buy the lie every time. Isn't that the secret of stereotypes?"

While he was speaking, a new receptionist wandered into a nearby cubicle to report having seen him through the open window of Mrs. Wilberforce's pretty ground-floor apartment that morning, enjoying coffee and croissants at the compromising hour of seven. The news was dismissed by barely listening secretaries as unworthy of retailing.

"But he was wearing her bathrobe!" the receptionist protested.

"Don't you think that says something?" An executive secretary smirked.

And the receptionist was convinced against the evidence of her eyes, not so much by the catchy label "fag hag" as by the executive secretary's gold watch ("trust it till the end of time") and designer shoes ("the footwear that says you're going places").

Mrs. Wilberforce, however, did not believe in the protective power of her reputation. One day she opened the door of the ladies' room to hear a junior research associate saying ". . . sure there's something between them—" then fall abruptly silent at the sight of her. Mrs. Wilberforce was certain the sudden shutting-up could only mean that the young woman's words referred to herself and Mr. Palmer, although in fact the junior research associate had been speculating—accurately—about Ms. Kroesig and a new brand manager at a long-standing Blenheim client's, and had ceased speaking in the belief that Mrs. Wilberforce's longevity in Ms. Kroesig's service necessitated loyal tale-bearing.

Mrs. Wilberforce was disposed to panic. "We'll just have to stop seeing each other," she told Mr. Palmer. The only concession his ardent objections could evoke was "at least for a while."

Mr. Palmer was quick to point out that leaving her circle suddenly would be an indiscretion in itself: Of all the cliques at Blenheim, none spread gossip with greater gusto. So he was suffered to continue lunching, dining, and attending drag revues or classical concerts with her, provided they were chaperoned by at least one of the boys.

Lingering in conference rooms after meetings as though to exchange information about the details of a project, they sometimes found opportunities for a few words tête-à-tête. On one of these occasions, Mr. Palmer complained, "I am not enjoying my social life anymore. Popular though I am. Last night, after we saw you home, Walter made a pass at me."

"What did you do?"

"Oh, I stayed in character. 'Not tonight, darling, I have a headache.' That kind of thing is going to keep happening, though."

Flattening a prototype package, Mrs. Wilberforce said playfully, "Not forever. Once you get a few gray hairs . . ." He didn't smile. "Aren't you gay? At all?" It was a question she had often wanted, yet never brought herself, to ask at the time of their greater intimacy.

Mr. Palmer shook his head. "I sort of tried to be, once upon a time, but it was no use. It *would* be more convenient, wouldn't it? I seem to belong in that world in some ways, but I just couldn't manage that one crucial thing. So now you know." He shrugged uncomfortably.

"Have you considered therapy?" asked Mrs. Wilberforce, meaning it as a joke.

"Yes," Mr. Palmer told her. "That was no good, either."

"What you need," Mrs. Wilberforce muttered eventually, "is a Bruce."

"I never heard that term for it," Mr. Palmer said.

"*George's lover,*" Mrs. Wilberforce explained impatiently. "You know."

Mr. Palmer didn't. He shook his head.

"George is in love with a man who lives on the Coast. You must have seen the picture on George's desk."

"Oh, yeah. I thought it was just a pinup."

"Well, Bruce *is* a model. The thing is, George only sees him three or four times a year, but he's absolutely loyal, and everyone respects him for it. He says they're planning to settle down together when Bruce gets too old to work, and everyone thinks it's really touching. Everyone except Walter. He thinks the only thing that keeps George faithful is fear of AIDS."

"I don't like Walter," Mr. Palmer remarked.

"Oh, he's all right, really. He's awfully amusing."

"Awfully," Mr. Palmer nodded.

"He'd let you alone, if he thought you had a lover somewhere. And I could go out with you without being terrified all the time of Kiki finding out."

"You want me to start telling people I have a lover on the Coast," Mr. Palmer summarized.

"You can do better than that," Mrs. Wilberforce exhorted. "Let's put him in Europe."

Staggering under a pile of back issues of *The Progressive Grocer* and *Frozen Food Age*, the scandal-mongering junior research associate entered the conference room with other members of her department, who had a meeting scheduled there. Briskly, Mrs. Wilberforce handed a package flat to

Mr. Palmer. "Give some thought to it," she urged him, leaving, "and let me have the specs by the end of the day."

The Junior Creative Director wandered back to his office, locked the door, swept five projects off his drafting table, and began to design himself a lover. Magic Marker squeaked over drawing tissue. He observed that those of his cartoons that did not look like Mrs. Wilberforce tended to resemble her predecessor in his affections. He stopped sketching. "Western Europe," he wrote. "Glitzy job." Crossing this out, he replaced it with "Movies/Photography." On a memo pad, he saved up questions for collaborative discussion with Mrs. Wilberforce: "(1) How did we meet? (2) Why didn't I mention him before?" Returning to the tissue, he scrawled, "SYMPATHY—ailment, injury."

Back in her cubicle, the Assistant to the Vice President, Creative Communications, was working on similar lines. "Art world," she wrote nervously in tiny letters, her tablet half-hidden under a report she was supposed to be summarizing for Ms. Kroesig on seasonal sales variations in the salted-snack category. Beneath "art world," she wrote, "language NO ONE SPEAKS," circling the capitalized words for added emphasis. Inspiration flagging, she scanned the report until the phrase "competitors using kosher shortening" prompted her to add "religious (former monk?)" to the list on her tablet. She drew an arrow leading away from "SPEAKS" to the lower right quadrant of the page, where she wrote, "Danish, Dutch, Greek," pausing to put "Basque" above "Danish"; pausing again, she erased "Basque."

Since it was the custom at that time for many of Blenheim's gay personnel to roller-skate for an hour or two at the Roxy on Wednesday nights, Mr. Palmer concluded, as he dialed her number in vain at nine o'clock, that he would find her there. Heading for Chelsea on the subway, he recognized some of his fellow-travelers from previous Wednesday nights on wheels.

"Where were you last week?" a very tall black queen asked him flirtatiously.

"At home with my squeeze," Mr. Palmer told him pleasantly, practicing. "He doesn't skate."

The young hunk working the door at the Roxy did occasional paste-up work at Blenheim, and let Mr. Palmer in free. The men from the subway noticed, and objected; Mr. Palmer heard their querulous voices as he strode to the edge of the rink. Spotting Mrs. Wilberforce twirling by with Walter, he went back to get skates. He was lacing them up in front of the bar when George, bending over to be on a level with his face, greeted him. Gesturing toward Mrs. Wilberforce, whom Walter, skating backward in an evident trance of self-satisfaction, was now dragging by both hands, George said, "She told me about your boyfriend. So we're in the same boat—you should have told me."

Just then, the d.j. put on "It's Raining Men," and, as its thunderous opening was recognized, a shrieking stampede clumped down from the bleachers toward the rink, engulfing Mr. Palmer and George. Mr. Palmer was not a very good skater, and would not have chosen to launch himself in such a crowd. Furious with Mrs. Wilberforce, needing urgently to know the story she had evidently already started spreading, he couldn't even look for her: His whole being was absorbed in avoiding collision. Eventually, however, he was startled by an arm thrust through and wrapped around his own: It was hers. At first speechless with rage and distress, he revolved with her until he collected the strength to sputter, "How about putting me on your mailing list?"

"What?" she yelled over the music, which was swelling as the majority of the skaters began singing merrily along.

The song gave no sign of ending.

"Never mind," he howled. Wretchedly, doggedly, he shifted his weight with the beats.

"God bless Mother Nature," the skaters were bellow-

ing with the Weather Girls (formerly Two Tuns of Fun),
"she's a single woman, too."

"Like Paolo and fucking Francesca," Mr. Palmer muttered, but finally, miraculously, the song was over. A sig-
nificant segment of the skaters glided off the rink. He pulled
Mrs. Wilberforce with it. "We have to talk," he told her
heavily.

"Buy me a beer," she ordered him gently. "I don't
want to leave before they play the waltzes."

At her suggestion, they clumped precariously up to the
highest seat with their bottles. By the time they were halfway up, his rage had dissolved. After all, they were about
to straighten things out. Like an eagle, he surveyed the
skaters below him. He was filled, now, with a proprietary
pride in Mrs. Wilberforce, the only woman in the whole
crowded place. Contentedly, he swigged as she did. He
recognized the black queen from the subway, gliding far
below like a particularly elegant young swan.

"I *had* to tell George," Mrs. Wilberforce began explaining. "We'd all stopped at the Empire to grab a ham-
burger on the way over, and he started talking about Bruce.
It was such a perfect opportunity—really, it would have
been spitting in the face of Providence to let it go by. I
just kind of got the ball rolling; I said you hadn't told me
very much, so we can still work most of it out together. I
even said I couldn't remember his name."

"Jesus Christ," said Mr. Palmer then, as the orderly
revolutions below were replaced by an unnerving spectacle.
Walter, easily spottable in his bright red T-shirt, dropped
to his knees, and the skaters behind him were piling over
like dominoes. The black swan sprawled backward, his
long legs splaying sideways where they tripped a couple
who were making prudently for the outermost edge of the
rink.

"He lost a contact lens," Mr. Palmer heard from one
of the seats a few feet farther down.

Mrs. Wilberforce had risen to her feet for a better view.

"Contact nothing," she said excitedly. "Someone broke a little old bottle of amyl nitrate down there."

The fallen were righting themselves with varying degrees of difficulty. Mr. Palmer saw one of them grab Walter's beard. The burly instructor who doubled as bouncer glided purposefully through the catastrophe, clearing the rink.

Mrs. Wilberforce, still standing, leaned forward trying to see more. As the wheels of her skates began turning under her, she collapsed hastily onto Mr. Palmer's lap. Laughing, he hugged her. "What a show!"

She leaned her head back into his shoulder, snuggling luxuriously, but in a moment she was sliding away, wriggling free of his arms. "Don't want to blow our cover when I spent the whole afternoon thinking it up," she explained. Since Mr. Palmer did not release her at once, she added seriously, "Hey—I could never get another job, you know."

The next day, many topics competed for the attention of gossiping Blenheim. The grapevine sagged, groaning under the weight of its ripe autumnal burdens, but continued to carry the news. Always a center of unofficial intelligence, the Word Processing Department, handicapped though it was by the incapacitation of its swiftest operator (for Walter's right hand had been cut on the broken bottle, and his left wrist sprained as he fell), disseminated revelations along with its memos and reports. Blenheim had lost one of its most remunerative accounts when the brand manager had tired of Ms. Kroesig's high-handed ways. By five o'clock, even the most out-of-it junior account executives knew that the agency was in the throes of one of its frequent reorganizations, and that pink slips would be discovered in some of the next day's paycheck envelopes. The administrative assistants they shared mentioned the casualties of the roller-disco too, hinting gleefully at unspeakable debaucheries. It now appeared that the stuck-up Junior Creative Director was wanted for questioning by Interpol in connection with the smuggling of icons forged by his crippled lover, a situation that the word processors did not expect to prevent the President of Blenheim from elevating Mr. Palmer to Vice President, Creative Direction.

That was because the eavesdropping operator had been obliged to leave his listening post just as the Executive Vice President, Creative Direction (immediate supervisor of both Junior Creative Director and Vice President, Creative Communications), had put the case for Mr. Palmer as the most suitable candidate for the new Vice Presidency, a position that would consolidate the responsibilities of Junior Creative Director with those of the now-disgraced (the very title was to be abolished) Vice President, Creative Communications.

The President of Blenheim, however, had dismissed the suggestion of his Executive Vice President, Creative Direction. "Out of the frying pan!" he had scoffed, presidentially. "I am not putting a queer in that spot and that is final." In the square of the proposed org. chart where the Executive Vice President, Creative Direction, had penciled "Palmer," the President's heavy pen printed "WILBERFORCE."

"She has a lot of talent," the Executive Vice President, Creative Direction, conceded, "but no background, no experience."

The President shook his head. "Ms. Kroesig," he pointed out bitterly, "had a very impressive resume. That Wilberforce woman, now, I've had my eye on her. She ran the department when Kroesig was on vacation: Things were never smoother. And she has a real flair for liquor. I see that as being very important to us in the next three years, especially with sports medicine down the tubes."

The Executive Vice President, Creative Direction, resigned himself to the presidential will. It was true, so far as he knew, that Mrs. Wilberforce's most creative communications to date had been in the alcoholic beverage category.

*   *   *

At the news of Ms. Kroesig's dismissal, a number of
Blenheim employees raised their voices in a spontaneous
chorus of "Ding-dong, the witch is dead," and most of
Mrs. Wilberforce's friends were among the singers. Mrs.
Wilberforce wore her laurels jauntily. Mr. Palmer, squeez-
ing her knee under conference tables all over the country,
had many opportunities to enjoy his special relationship
with the only woman in a roomful of men.

For six weeks, a letter from a repentant Mr. Wilberforce
stayed stubbornly in the "in" box on the desk of the new
Vice President, Creative Direction. Almost daily, Mrs.
Wilberforce reread the remorseful words of the man who,
in a moment of midlife madness, had left her after seventeen
years of marriage for a twenty-one-year-old girl. Mrs. Wilberforce was of an exceptionally forgiving nature, but on
the day Blenheim sent her, with Mr. Palmer (they had been
observed to represent the agency most successfully in tan-
dem), to plan a campaign at the headquarters of Europe's
leading manufacturer of men's underwear, she made up her
mind. Sitting cosily with Mr. Palmer that evening in a drag
bar in Montparnasse, she had scribbled on the back of a
picture postcard of the Eiffel Tower:

>How're ya gonna keep 'em
>Down on the farm
>After they've seen gay Paree?

MUCH ADO IN MUSHI-JI

FOR DANIEL MENAKER

Cathy's coming back, and there isn't
a female in Mushi-ji who hasn't heard
this news. Of course, not all of them took it in: Nakagawa
Fumie, for example, the town's oldest resident at 104, whose
great-great-granddaughter told her, having heard about it
at school. Or Kameda Midori, the town's youngest resident
at six days, whose grandmother mentioned it to the baby's
mother on their way to the public bathhouse. Fumie and
Midori reacted identically, lolling their bald heads back and
opening their toothless mouths meaninglessly.

But Jyaki-O, the Tanakas' Afghan bitch (named for
Jacqueline Onassis in acknowledgment of her elegance),
growled meanly and began thumping her tail nervously on
the ground when one of the little Tanaka girls told her
older sister while they were brushing their pet under the
scraggly mimosa tree in their disgraceful garden. No doubt
the dog felt the girls' distress: They were, no doubt, du-
plicating their mother's agitation.

To most of the housewives in Mushi-ji, the news is no more interesting than the much-advertised upcoming guest appearance of the rock duo Pink Lady on their favorite noon-time soap opera. Some of them plan to take Cathy's arrival as an occasion to speak sternly to their daughters about the decadent influence of the West, which they enjoy doing. Others look forward to simply laughing at Cathy's excesses.

Members of the neighborhood association of the third *chome*, the district where Cathy used to live, are, to a woman, dithering. And enjoying doing so. How, they wonder, can they do justice to Cathy's reappearance? It's a major event for Mushi-ji, where Cathy has celebrity standing. Before Cathy's arrival, none of its residents had any personal experience of an alien culture in all its riotous otherness. Then Cathy's husband had come to teach English at a university in Yokohama. This university owned a house in the third *chome* of Mushi-ji, and rented it to visiting professors. At the very least, Cathy's neighbors had found her immensely entertaining. They had enjoyed knowing her. She had furnished endless confirmations of their sense of Japan's unique superiority.

Except for Keiko Tanaka. No woman in Mushi-ji knew Cathy as well as she did, and none was influenced as she was. Besides bringing Mrs. Tanaka's English to a kind of fluency, Cathy so Americanized her that she is now considered not quite respectable.

Mrs. Tanaka, contemplating Cathy's arrival, simultaneously chain-smokes and bites her nicotine-stained nails. She has forgotten to comb her hair: The shaggy bangs, falling in her eyes, intensify her resemblance to her dog. She has reason to be disturbed, but her reaction is not extraordinary: She is absentminded at the best of times, and never calm.

She is worried about the confrontation she anticipates. It will be great to see her old friend again, of course (she thinks in English: "just great"). But her old friend from America will be seeing her new friend from America too, and that's the trouble.

Her new friend is not really so new, having lived for the

past six years in the house where Cathy lived before her, which is where we will have to go to see the most extreme response in Mushi-ji to the news of Cathy's imminent visit.

Remove your shoes, Reader, before you cross the threshold. The Lerners live there now, Edith and Herb. In Cathy's day, sneakers may have violated the tatami, but not in Edith's. This *is* a Japanese house, after all, and Edith is determined to do right by it. She believes, too, that it behooves her as a respectable matron to maintain her cool at all times, or at the very least to appear decently *heki* (serene—more or less), whatever may be raging within her, but it's no good now: She's lost it.

In fact, her heart is so full that, although experience suggests that doing so will only make her feel worse, she has begun to tell her husband about it. Even as she speaks, she regrets doing so, but she can't seem to stop herself. Unluckily for Edith, this discussion is taking place in the bedroom, which is full of mirrors. Wherever Edith turns, she sees a woman who cannot compete with Cathy's flamboyant exoticity. Cathy is Mushi-ji's idea of a properly *foreign* foreigner, and Edith has, in her six years' residence, heard a little more than she can (at the moment) bear to know about Cathy's golden curls, about her Mediterranean curves, about her Scandinavian height, and about her American informality. Edith has had to exclaim politely over many photographs of Cathy, for every house in the third *chome* has at least one of them and most of Edith's neighbors have lots of them: Cathy in fringed, embroidered, bell-bottomed jeans; Cathy in psychedelic Pucci-print miniskirts; Cathy in exiguous jersey tops that make Edith blush for her country, since it is evident in the photographs that she is not wearing a bra, and really, with a figure like that, she should be.

As for Edith, those mirrors are showing her hair as straight as her figure and as black as her eyes. She stands five two in her highest heels. Her neighbors tell her, "Except for the shape of your eyes and nose, you could be one of us," good-naturedly regarding her nearly Japanese appearance as an oddity in itself, since it is the only one Edith gives them to exclaim over.

Edith's deportment, back in America, was modeled on that of her mother, who until her divorce was the most punctilious woman in the stuffiest town on the eastern seaboard. In Japan, Edith has devoted herself with compulsive energy to mastering every nuance of Japanese etiquette. Within four years, she could use correctly all the verb forms that indicate the difference in social status between the speaker, the addressed, and the spoken-about. Within five years, she could—and did—change the angle and the timing of her bow to convey properly augmented respect to the wife of Judge Nishimura; not that she stinted the wife of Dr. Yamamoto —who, with three sons at Tokyo University, was entitled to, and got, a bit more than the wife of Dr. Yamada.

The correctness of her deportment is not in evidence at the moment.

"Herbie," she is wailing, "you don't understand."

"Sure I do," Herb tells her. "You've been such a big fish in this little pond. You're afraid this Cassie is a bigger fish, and naturally you—"

"No, you know what? It turns out her name is actually *Cathy*. I'd never seen it written till yesterday. All this time I thought it was Cassie—because they say Cashi, you know?" To her mortification, Edith feels tears spilling out of her eyes, and turns to the window to avoid seeing them in any of the mirrors.

"Cathy, then," says Herb. "I wonder if she'll think our name is *Rana*. . . ."

"Herbie!" Edith squeals, "She is some kind of *hippie!* She planted marijuana in the Tanaka's garden." Edith peers around at her husband through her tears to see whether he is impressed. To her disgust, he appears to be disguising amusement, and not even troubling to disguise it well. After a histrionic pause, Edith comes out with what she has been saving: "She's coming here with her *lover*."

Herb shrugs. He meets his wife's flattened mouth and

streaming eyes with an exasperated outflow of breath. "Edie, it's none of your business."

"They're going to want me to have her in this house. Doesn't that make it my business? And there *is* a principle at stake," Edith insists. "She's a married woman; she has three *children*, Herb; she's already given everyone a terrible impression of our country. . . ."

"I didn't get such a good impression of it myself, Edie. I chose to leave," Herb reminds her.

"She was a terrible influence on Keiko Tanaka—you know that's true. Those poor little girls . . . The point is—" Edith chokes on her emotions.

"The point is your *consequence,* as Jane Austen would call it. Your importance. Admit it."

"You don't understand, Herb," Edith says for the second time in five minutes.

Jane Austen is never far from the top of Herb's mind these days. "You think you've got problems, Edith. I've marked fourteen of my seniors' papers on *Persuasion* this afternoon. Eight of them start with the same paragraph, which, as it happens, is the first paragraph of the foreword to the text we used. Four of the papers are word-for-word identical. It's hopeless, hopeless . . . there's no concept of intellectual property in Japan. You can't even make them understand why it's wrong . . . and I gave them that book because I thought they'd have no trouble understanding it." He looks at Edith as though for comfort, although that is not what he expects from her.

"I'd better start dinner," she mutters, subdued by the suspicion that her husband might be at least partly right about why she doesn't want to see Cathy.

The neighbors are beginning to find Edith a little irritating. At first, her studious imitativeness was quite flattering, and refreshing after three years of Cathy's self-confident brashness. But the relentless correctness of Edith's demeanor is a passive reproach to them. And then, there was

The Incident, when the reproach became active. Saintly Mrs. Ishibashi is discussing it now (for it is still controversial) with flashy Mrs. Teramoto, who makes her nervous. They are on their way to the Tanakas'.

"Rana-San [Mrs. Lerner: Edith] went too far," Mrs. Teramoto asserts, raising her hand and extending it in a gesture intended to indicate going too far. The gesture also displays the gold-bangle watch that all Mushi-ji agrees is in the worst possible taste.

"Perhaps it was not intended," Mrs. Ishibashi suggests.

"Since it was in no way necessary for her to refer to the Tanakas' dog . . ." Mrs. Teramoto trails off, which is how polite conversations are conducted by Japanese ladies.

"But perhaps she thought it would be rude to change the subject?" Mrs. Ishibashi persists in defense of Edith, whom she loves.

"She can only have said it to cause Mrs. Ueda to lose face," Mrs. Teramoto declares. "I wonder if Rana-San thinks it is wrong for us to give so much deference to Mrs. Ueda. Americans don't approve of geisha: I don't know much about Americans, I am thankful to say, but I know that."

"But it is because Mrs. Ueda was a geisha that she understands etiquette so thoroughly. It could be seen that she was humiliated . . ." and Mrs. Ishibashi, remembering Mrs. Ueda's pained, startled expression, gives an anguished hiss, for she loves Mrs. Ueda, too. That is the nature of her saintliness: No one, from her unlovable husband to unknowable barbarians in countries she has never even heard of, is exempt from her affection.

"All the more humiliated because no one humiliates the wife of Mr. Ueda, isn't that so?"

Mrs. Teramoto's question is conventional, rhetorical: Mrs. Ishibashi's feelings are spared the ordeal of trying to frame an answer that will not outrage her love for either of the women being discussed.

And this conversation is taking place because Mrs. Ueda used a certain verb form in mentioning the Tanakas' dog, and Edith then referred to the dog using another, arguably more proper, verb form. Of course, Edith was too well behaved to correct Mrs. Ueda's usage directly, but even so, public opinion, ripe for an excuse to do so, had turned against Edith.

Mrs. Teramoto and Mrs. Ishibashi have reached the bottom of the hill. They cross the Tanakas' disorderly, neglected front yard, exchanging a glance of disapproval at its condition. They slide open the Tanakas' front door and say "*Gomen kudasai*," which is what people do in Japan instead of ringing doorbells. Then they linger in front of the threshold waiting for someone to give them permission to cross it, and to bring them slippers. From the foyer, they can see Mrs. Tanaka slumped over her kitchen table, surrounded by dirty dishes, smoking and reading a book in English, which is propped up on the electronic rice cooker. The sight evokes another wordless sharing of disapproval.

Hearing her visitors, Mrs. Tanaka rises, approaches, and sinks to the floor to welcome them in a listless and perfunctory way that Mrs. Ishibashi thinks sadly is setting a very bad example for the Tanaka daughters. Mrs. Ishibashi's pity only increases her fondness for slatternly, rebellious, Americanized Mrs. Tanaka, who offers her guests dusty slippers. And, really, the visitors have not even sunk into a full kneeling position on the cushions she pulls out for them before, with barbarous abruptness, she announces, "You have come because of Cathy." (No one called Cathy "Mrs. Campbell," because she never permitted it.)

Mrs. Ishibashi, who likes conversations to be led into at a seemly pace, with remarks about the weather and inquiries about family members, becomes sadder still. Mrs. Teramoto is cheered by Mrs. Tanaka's unladylike briskness, which affirms her conviction of her own superiority. (Mrs. Teramoto may have her faults, but she knows how to start a conversation.)

"Having been such a great friend of Cathy's, naturally . . ." Mrs. Teramoto implies, pushing back the sleeve of her cardigan to flash the deplorable watch.

"Since you are a friend of both of the foreign ladies . . ." Mrs. Ishibashi joins in implication.

"Of course, I will try," Mrs. Tanaka tells them, lighting a cigarette although one is already burning in the ashtray in front of her, "but I know Edith will not want to have Cathy in her house."

"I don't understand," says Mrs. Ishibashi. "Since it is the house where Cathy lived, herself, it is only natural to invite her there. Not to do so would be impolite."

"You see, Cathy seems to Edith . . ." Mrs. Tanaka falters, because although she is speaking Japanese, the only words that come to her now are English ones. It occurs to her that she has learned most of them from Edith: "objectionable," for example. The English she learned from Cathy didn't seem to have any words for disapproval.

"It doesn't seem as if they came from the same country, does it?" Mrs. Teramoto asks rhetorically.

"Foreigners!" all the ladies exclaim together, and share a giggle over the strangeness of the world outside Japan, and the particular strangeness of the country that sent them the atom bomb, and the occupation, and Cathy, and Edith, and "I Love Lucy."

"So it's decided," Mrs. Teramoto says in a little while.

Mrs. Tanaka interrupts an exhalation of smoke with one of her racking coughs. "Rana-San will have Cathy to tea, with us and Mrs. Mikimoto and Mrs. Suzuki, after all of us have lunch at Mrs. Ishibashi's."

Mrs. Tanaka knows it won't be easy, though. And when her husband staggers over the threshold at 1:30 A.M., he finds her still smoking at the kitchen table. As a general rule, she is the only wife in the neighborhood who doesn't wait up for her husband. In fact, she is so Westernized that she doesn't even get up to make his breakfast, so that weeks have sometimes passed when she has seen him only on the weekends. Although he has had the whole train ride from Tokyo to sober up, he is still a little drunk, and the sight of her slumped over the dirty dishes fills him with tenderness.

She tells him what's bothering her. He doesn't really understand, but he can see she's worried and he respects her grasp of foreigners' ways. "I suppose that's what you should expect for getting mixed up with Americans, though," he says, but sympathetically. He's an easygoing guy. If he wasn't, he would have straightened her out—or, failing that, divorced her—years ago. He persuades her to join him in the bath, where they soak in companionable silence, she brooding over how to persuade Edith to entertain Cathy, he taking some pride in having a wife with such sophisticated problems.

The next day Herb Lerner comes home, slides open the front door, and flings his briefcase on the threshold in disgust, for it contains (he has discovered on the train) four more identical papers about *Persuasion* as well as *The Britannica's* article on "Austen, Jane," transcribed not very accurately in beautiful calligraphy and bright turquoise ink. His mood is bad; it worsens as, bending to untie his shoes, he hears Tanaka Keiko's voice, and then his wife's. He knows other Americans who are working in Japan. Their wives' involvement with Japanese culture goes no deeper than teaching English part-time and learning enough Japanese to shop with, maybe taking a few classes in flower-arranging. He doesn't know why Edith has chosen to turn herself into a Japanese housewife, and he really hates coming home to find the house full of dumpy little neighbors who bob up and down at the sight of him and burst into nervous giggles at whatever he says, covering their mouths like the modest creatures they are.

Mrs. Tanaka, actually, does none of these things, but somehow he finds his heart sinking at the thought of having to hear her determinedly idiomatic English. ("So, Professor, how is the world treating you?" "You look all in." "I am crazy about Wordsworth." All these things she said, the last time he saw her.) She's the only one there with Edith, he realizes, because the language he's overhearing is English, and just as he begins lacing up his shoe again, figuring he can go out and look at the fish pond for a while where the women can't see him from the dining room—which is where their voices seem to be coming from—he begins to listen to what his wife is saying.

". . . so that, gradually, the state of California has be-come a kind of ghetto—like a Bunraku, you know—for crazy people."

"I am not quite digging how this can be," Mrs. Tanaka complains.

"Oh, Keiko, I've told you about saying 'dig'—believe me, it sounds foolish. You learned that from Cathy, didn't you?"

"I think so."

"Well, it proves my point."

"I am sure I have read it in some books, people saying 'dig,' meaning 'understand.' "

Mrs. Tanaka's voice sounds sullen.

"But what *sort* of people?" Edith asks her. "Suppose I started using gangsters' slang when I spoke Japanese, Keiko?"

"What is 'gangsters'?"

"*Yakuza,*" Edith translates impatiently.

"But Cathy's husband is professor of English, like your husband," Mrs. Tanaka says.

"That doesn't mean the same thing in America that it means in Japan," says Edith. "I don't want to meet this woman, much less entertain her. She smokes pot; she gave you drugs—that's against the law, and *very wrong.*"

"Is it really so very bad?" Keiko wants to know.

"Yes, it is," Edith tells her.

Now Mrs. Tanaka tries the strategy she evolved in the bathtub last night. "In spite of that, you should ask her to tea. It is expected of you."

Herb strains to hear his wife's answer. It is long in coming.

"If Mrs. Teramoto brought her lover here, would you have them to tea?"

"Of course," Mrs. Tanaka answers. "Why not? You know, when Cathy lived here, many people thought I had love affair with her husband. So everyone asked me to lunch! Always! I did not make my own lunch for three weeks—I was so popular. They felt sorry for me, or they thought it was very interesting."

"Keiko?" Edith's voice is at its gentlest. "When people

are unkind to you—and even to your daughters—is that why, really? Because they think you were carrying on with Cathy's husband?"

Mrs. Tanaka's laughter turns to coughing. "That is because I wear jeans, because I smoke, and don't clean the house, things like that. 'Carrying on' means having love affair?"

"It can," Edith tells her. "Keiko?"

"You are thinking that, too! But I have never had love affair, only with my husband before we are married, because it was necessary."

"How do you mean, 'necessary'?" Edith wonders.

"My parents are making a marriage for me with some nice, rich kind of man. But I am already in love with Tetsuyo, I don't want that marriage. So that is how we stop it; we got Atsuko." (Atsuko is the oldest of the Tanakas' daughters.)

"So you were always so . . . defiant."

"Yes," Mrs. Tanaka says, sounding smug. "Even in my girlhood, I always defy. I think that is why I am Cathy's friend. Why I love to learn English, why I love when she tells me about America. But then, when you come, I think you are telling me about some other country. And then, when I read some books, I think America is like Cathy tells me, and then when I read some other books, I think America is like what you tell me.

"I have not tell you this before. But I wrote to Cathy about you, and she wrote to me you are 'snooty' and 'uptight'—I have not know these words before—and there are not many people like you in America, and now you tell me Cathy is a crazy and a criminal, and there are not many people like Cathy in America. And I don't dig—understand—how this can be. In Japan, when maybe somebody very old-fashioned is talking about Japan with somebody very progressing, maybe one is saying they like something and the other is saying they don't like it, but they are talking about the same Japan. But I have listen to you and to Cathy, and I have read many books and magazines and seen many movies, and I don't know what kind of place is America."

Herb, eavesdropping, is really interested in hearing what Edith will say, although he's not in the habit of taking her seriously.

"Keiko, do you know the word 'pluralistic'?"

There has been no reason to mention it before, but Tanaka Keiko can't pronounce the letter "l," and she can't recognize it, either. Being, as she sometimes says, "a good sport," she ventures a guess.

"I know!" Mrs. Tanaka cries. "Having a swimming pool? Or *like* some swimming pool?"

"In America," Edith tells her patiently, abandoning the guessing game, "people are more different from each other than they are in Japan. There are more different kinds of people. There is nothing to stop them from . . . from experimenting with the way they live. And, Keiko, it is not good.

"My own family, Keiko. They used to keep all the rules, and when I was little, everyone felt sorry for me because my parents were so strict. Then my father started . . . experimenting. Gave up his job all of a sudden, left my mother, moved to the west coast, married a much younger woman. My mother just fell apart completely, started to drink . . . my little brothers sort of fell apart too, then . . . drugs and . . .

"The point is, it couldn't have happened in Japan, Keiko. All this freedom doesn't make people happy. People are much happier in Japan."

"But in Japan, maybe a woman suicides herself if it happen to her like to your mother. People are not suiciding themselves so much in America," Mrs. Tanaka points out.

"But you wouldn't say that if you weren't so . . . so steeped in Western ideas."

"What is 'steeped'?"

"Soaked, like making tea. The point is, Mrs. Ishibashi wouldn't have said that. Mrs. Teramoto wouldn't have said that. Keiko, here in Japan, when anyone's badly floundering, they have to straighten out or die. It's ruthless, but it works. America leaves everyone free to flounder for their whole life, and it doesn't work. Everyone suffers in the end."

Herb hears Mrs. Tanaka's voice, sullen again: "Flounder is fish."

Herb is furious as his wife switches to Japanese. He catches no more than a word or two in each sentence. Eventually, though, there is a pause, after which Mrs. Tanaka says, in English, "I am not so good Japanese, and I think you are not so good American, you should *tolerate* Cathy. But you *defy,* you are more like me than you think you are, because if you are good Japanese—like you tell me you want to be—you *obey* to what the neighborhood association of third *chome* decides, and you invite Cathy to tea in this house. But you obey only to your conscience, you are American after all and I see you are like Cathy."

And Herb hears the *shoji* doors of the dining room sliding open, and grabs his briefcase and scurries off to the fish pond, and from there he sees Mrs. Tanaka emerge from the front door and reach the front-yard entrance gate, and he sees Edith explode out of the house and dash across the yard (in house slippers!) and hears her tell Mrs. Tanaka, "All right! All right! You win, damn it, I'll have her to tea."

And he hears Mrs. Tanaka say, "Three cheers for you! I will tell Mrs. Ishibashi."

Cathy isn't coming, after all, and there isn't a female in Mushi-ji who hasn't heard this news. Her lover renounced her; instead of taking Cathy to Japan, he is taking his wife and children to Yosemite in a Winnebago. But, just as the cancellation of a summit conference that might have been expected to headline the front page of the paper may be pushed as far back as the bottom of page two by the apprehension of a spy, Cathy's nonarrival seems scarcely worth mentioning what with Edith's imminent departure to discuss. The neighborhood association of the third *chome* meets to decide where the farewell party will be held.

"My house is right across the street," Mrs. Ishibashi points out, "And I taught her to bow." She is a little tearful as she adds, "And I will miss her so much."

Mrs. Teramoto, glancing at the infamous watch as though checking the time—which everyone is well aware she has no need to do what with the huge clock mounted on the wall she is facing—declares: "My house is right next door, and of a much more suitable size, considering that we'll have to ask *everybody*."

"It is my fault she is going," Mrs. Tanaka announces, gloomily lighting one cigarette with another.

"It is her husband's fault," Mrs. Teramoto says.

"If I had not said what I said, she would not have said what she said. It was because he heard her say that, that he decided not to renew his contract," Mrs. Tanaka tells her, "so it is my fault, and I should give the party." (Reader? Since she is speaking Japanese now, she says all this without using a single personal pronoun. I just thought you might like to know.)

"Even if that is true," Mrs. Ishibashi remarks, "it is all for the best. I am very sorry she is going, but really she has been in Japan too long."

"Her husband said so." Mrs. Tanaka sighs.

"Mrs. Ueda's house is the most suitable; it is such a pity about That Incident . . ." Mrs. Ishibashi says.

And in the end, perhaps in tribute to the pluralism they expect will reabsorb Edith, they decide to follow lunch at Mrs. Ishibashi's with dessert at Mrs. Teramoto's, then wind up with tea and beer at Mrs. Tanaka's. And so, although neither of them shows any sign of knowing what is happening, ancient Mrs. Nakagawa is wheeled to the Tanakas', and tiny Miss Kameda is carried, to bid the Lerners farewell on the day of their departure. Jyaki-O wags her tail wildly with what looks like joy, but there is no reason to suppose she is glad to see Edith go. No doubt she is pleased because so many people are feeding her cookies and *o-sembei*, her two favorite treats, which she has never before eaten at the same time.

OUR HEARTS WERE OLD AND GRAY

FOR JAY BRADY

I was facing into my fortieth birthday, and I was taking stock, as people do when they realize their lives are at least half over and they haven't accomplished a damn thing. I was asking myself what I'd wasted all those years on, anyway, and the answer I came up with was: sex. So I decided to cut it right out of my life just like *that*. Cold turkey.

I wouldn't recommend celibacy for everybody, but I will say this for it: It saves a lot of time. When I think of the years I wasted . . . oh, well. Spilt milk butters no parsnips.

I'm *much* happier this way. I realize now that for most of my life I was living a lie, struggling to fit into the prepackaged identity society had prepared for me, when all along I was a latent asexual.

I should have suspected years ago, I guess, but it's not

the sort of thought that occurs to you. At least, not in the circles I move in.

Everybody I know insists that they *need* sex. And they go on insisting, even when their lives are nothing but a string of erotically caused disasters. Take my friend Polly. Short, I think, for Polymorphous Perversity, since her real name is Maria. There's nothing and no one she hasn't tried, including me.

And what has she got to show for it? She started out, when we were in college together, as a really promising painter, but she got sidetracked into being an art moll. I tell her it's not too late to get her act together, but she won't even *consider* it.

Last spring, I was going to take her to Paris. I couldn't really afford it, but I thought it would be good for her— looking at a lot of art and architecture, with somebody (me) with her best interests at heart, who didn't just want to use her. I do love Polly; she's the best friend I've ever had. And watching her becoming this pathetic *thing,* this middle-aged art groupie, was really getting painful for me.

We were meeting in a restaurant in SoHo for lunch. I was late—I had to wait forever for a downtown train. She was sitting on a stool at the bar. I remember thinking she was losing her looks before my very eyes.

I embraced her, clumsily, so that the bar stool teetered a little. I kissed the air under her earring because my lipstick was fresh. "Have you been waiting long?" I asked, hoping she would lie and say no, although I could see her glass was nearly empty.

"Roz—I actually didn't recognize you in that wig," she told me. "Is it new?"

"No, no, you've seen it before—but maybe not on me."

"Huh?" Her blue eyes, still beautiful, startlingly round, roamed analytically over the wig. "Did I see it in Canal Jeans?"

"Maybe," I told her, unable to remember where I got

it. "But what I meant was that you'd probably seen it in my apartment."

Again, her beautiful eyes appraised my head. "It looks different on a wig stand," she said.

"Do I add or detract?" I asked her, but I wasn't sure I really wanted her to tell me. She only grinned, so I explained, "I always feel like such a *dork* if I come to SoHo dressed normally. Know what I mean?"

"Those pants . . ." she muttered, nodding very solemnly at the lower half of me. I guess I'm not very good at the SoHo look.

"Since I didn't have to go to work this morning—" I said, trying to distract her from my failure of a costume.

"You spent all morning deciding what to wear?" she sneered. "And you came up with *that*?"

I thumbed my nose at her. "I love you, too," I said. "No, *listen*, it's Good Friday, that's why I have the day off. So I stumbled on this church—it's called St. Esprit—where they were having this service *in French*."

"You went to *church*?" Polly was really sneering, not just kidding around. "Roz, that's The Enemy. I hope you won't mind my saying this, but you're getting really peculiar, you know that?"

"Polly, I wasn't *worshiping* anything. I just wanted to see if I could follow the French. And I *could*. Listen, baby, I'm going to show you Paris—"

"Let's get a table," Polly suggested suddenly, dismounting. I felt envious as she stood there in her paint-smeared jeans and sweatshirt. Like a native costume. I almost expected the waitress to show me a tourist menu.

The one she brought, though, listed many forms of overpriced alfalfa sprouts. Depressed, I told her, "We'll start with white wine." She began to recite the vintages that could be obtained by the glass, but I cut her off. "The house white." I watched her wander off: She belonged in SoHo too, but almost too much so. In six years, I thought, she'll have gone back home to the midwest; she'll be picking her kids up from day care in a station wagon full of crayons and fast-food containers.

"How did you know I wasn't drinking Château Déshabillé?" Polly wondered, derailing my train of thought.

"My dear," I told her, "I've known you for at least twenty-five years—isn't that a sobering thought?"

"Sure is," Polly muttered.

"Well, have you found a good pair of museum shoes?" I asked her.

"Rozzie?"

Her tone gave me pause. It *boded*, if you know what I mean. I furrowed my brow. The wine arrived, and I raised my glass. "To Paris," I toasted. "Oh, Polly, remember that book they used to make everyone read in high school, 'cause it was just such wholesome fun? Called *Our Hearts Were Young and Gay*? I think it was by Cornelia—"

"Oh, Roz," Polly said. She was playing with her silverware. She wouldn't look up at me.

"Yes?" I said after a year or two.

"I—I don't think I want to go anymore. Maybe later. But not now."

I lowered my glass. "But—" I actually sputtered. "Do you know how long I've been planning this? Scrimping and saving? And I've spent *every spare moment* for the past six months brushing up my French. I recite irregular verbs while I do my tummy exercises! I read a Sévigné letter every morning while I eat my breakfast! And clearing the time for my vacation—do you have any idea how they hate it if you change your plans, where I work?"

"Yeah," Polly whispered forlornly, still not looking up. "And it's worse than that, Roz. I called the charter place. We can't get our money back. But I really . . ." She raised those guileless blue eyes again, looked around the restaurant, and faced me, finally. "I really don't want to go now. My parents called, begged me not to. My brother, too."

* * *

I took some wine, held it on my tongue. It tasted somehow both harsh and vapid. It seemed like a good idea to make friends with it, though: I suspected I was going to be drinking a lot of it before the afternoon was over. "Might one inquire *why*?" I asked Polly, eventually.

"Well," she said, "the danger. I mean, it's not like we *have* to go. It's just a vacation. We're going for *fun*. How could we have fun, anyway, with bombs going off all over the place? Even if I didn't believe it was that dangerous, I don't think I could have much fun with my family worried sick about me the whole time."

That's the only concession Polly's made to middle age: She made peace with her family.

"Danger!" I screeched indignantly. "It's a highly subjective thing, danger. You scare me to death all the time, think nothing of getting on the subway in the middle of the night in the most terrifying neighborhoods. You amaze me, you really do. I can't expect your family to be immune to journalism, but you—you're a sensible woman, Polly, you know better."

"How do you mean, 'immune to journalism'? The news isn't a *lie;* there really have been bombs going off in Paris. I read about a hundred people have been *maimed* in the last four months."

"Oh, that's what I mean," I told her. "That's sensationalism; when people are maimed by terrorist bombs, someone tots up the statistics. How many people do you think have been maimed, or killed, for that matter, by violent criminals in New York in the last four months? *That* statistic isn't part of some ongoing news story, nobody's going to bother *enumerating*. Polly, I'll bet you if some impersonal actuary was estimating our chances of survival in the next month, we'd have better odds in Paris than we would right here. Especially *you*! I don't just mean running all over New York at all hours, but when I think of some of the people you sleep with—"

Polly looked hurt, and annoyed. "Why can't we just *postpone* the trip?"

"Till when?" I wondered.

"Till it's *safer*," she said impatiently.

"It may never be safer! The world gets worse all the time. Haven't you noticed? It's just too bad that reasonable people like us have no interest in running it. Perhaps we should step in. I mean, when that madman in the White House is feeling old and weak, he starts moving battleships. Poises his finger on the button. When we're feeling old and weak, we buy perfume. I don't know, Polly, what do you think? Shouldn't we take over?"

I was losing my cool, trying to win her back. She came up with a horribly weak smile. I thought I could feel my heart sinking. It was a distinct physical sensation, like when you finally succeed in washing down a lump of peanut butter with a good swig of milk.

"Let's order lunch," Polly suggested. "They have some very good salads here."

" 'They have very good salads here,' " I repeated. "Jesus. You sound like one of my French tapes. Well, I can't face a salad on an empty stomach. Let's have another *plonc*." I signaled the waitress and pointed to our glasses, just as if I was too sophisticated to be furious.

"Is there any good reason why we can't just go later?" Polly wanted to know.

"I can think of several *excellent* reasons why we shouldn't. For one thing, you just told me we can't get our money back."

"Roz, I really don't want to be melodramatic, but what's a couple of hundred dollars compared to, say, the loss of your eyesight?"

I couldn't very well tell Polly that this trip was supposed to save her from an inglorious middle age. "It's the principle of the thing," I said. "As far as I'm concerned, if you let the terrorists cancel your plans, you might as well be *colluding*. Giving them what they want. They'd like nothing better than if everyone refused to get on a plane till France lets a bunch *more* terrorists out of jail. The only way to stop terrorists is to ignore them. It's like a spoiled child. Give in whenever it has a tantrum, and you've no one but yourself to blame if you've raised a monster. It's only common sense, Polly," I said, coming to believe this argument as I made it, thinking: Lust is a terrorist.

"You can't compare bombs to tantrums!" she objected.

"But that's what they *are;* it's a matter of degree, that's all. Besides," I told her, craftily, "I'm going to be forty in May. I have no intention of turning forty without having seen Paris. It seems uncivilized."

She slapped the menu violently down on the table.

I waited, but she didn't say anything.

"*Our Hearts Were Young and Gay,*" I said. "Old and gray is more like it."

"Don't try to make me feel guilty!" Polly said. "It's not as if you hadn't been *everywhere* else."

I shrugged. "All right," I said, feeling abruptly as if I was admitting to something shameful. "I've traveled quite a bit. But it was really very *lackluster.* I lived in Thailand. Big deal. What my so-called travel boiled down to is nothing but back-and-forthing on the cheap. Stopovers in all the drabbest airports in the socialist bloc. Polly, stale sandwiches in Helsinki isn't the kind of memory that consoles you as you head into old age, believe me."

"Well, there you are." Polly flattened her mouth in sullen triumph. "You've flown too much. You're not even afraid of planes."

I couldn't deny it. "I'm terrified of cars, though," I offered. Polly was silent. I thought it would be tactless to allude again to the dangers of her sex life, so I carried on: "That seems more sensible. There are *lots* more car accidents than plane accidents. And you know how I feel about the subway."

Even as I said these things, I felt myself to be losing the argument. Some heartless bookkeeper in the back of my mind pointed out that half a double room *sans douche* was 48F, whereas a single was 72F. "Well, Polly," I said, "I think it's very silly of you to feel the way you do, but since that *is* the way you feel, I don't think you *should* go." That is the kind of relationship I have with the heartless bookkeeper in the back of my mind.

"I don't think *you* should go, either," Polly mumbled rather timidly.

"I appreciate your concern for my welfare," I informed her stiffly—though I *was* touched, "but canceling this trip, as I have just explained, would violate my principles. Besides, if I really thought there was any danger to speak of, I wouldn't have tried to persuade you to go. At this point, I'd rather go without you. I don't say that easily; you know how I hate eating alone in public. But suppose you're right: I can see us dropping to the boulevard 'mid the rockets' red glare, shrapnel whizzing around our ears, your last words to me 'I told you so.' An intolerable way to enter extinction."

"Can we order lunch?" Polly asked me plaintively. "This is my third glass of wine, you know."

"Yes, yes, we can order lunch. Sorry, Polly."

Looking around for the waitress, I spotted Roger Oistrach striding through the door with a woman wearing the same wig I was. Seeing Roger wasn't such an extraordinary coincidence; he lives and works in this neighborhood. After all, he introduced Polly to this restaurant. As for the wig, I had to ask myself whether my eye for SoHo style wasn't so far off. Could it be that in real life that woman dressed in the same drab clothes as I do? "Polly, look who's here."

The bewigged woman veered around the bar, in the direction of the toilets and telephones, and Roger, having spotted us, made for our table. I dislike Roger, an intermittent boyfriend of Polly's, for no good reason. He has a perfect right to practice art criticism. Broad shoulders are not incompatible with sound aesthetic judgment. I reminded myself of this, commending myself for my fair-mindedness, as he greeted us with his usual obnoxious heartiness.

"Polly and Roz!" He flattened his mouth and nodded, as though Polly, by appearing with me in public, had confirmed some unpleasant suspicion he'd had about her. He doesn't like me any more than I like him. I have no idea why; perhaps it's something chemical. "I almost didn't recognize you in that wig," he told me with the kind of condescendingly indulgent smile that provokes fistfights.

"I really should stop wearing it. You're starting to see them on *everyone*," I ventured, hoping I was being insulting to the woman he was with.

He didn't respond. Maybe she wasn't really with him, I thought, just happened to walk in the door at the same time.

"May I join you?" he asked. He was looking at Polly. My lips formed "no" but I didn't say it.

Polly had already cleared our bags and coats from the chair next to his. Roger lowered his bulk into it, rubbing his hands together. "So what's new?"

"We were about to go to Paris together, but I seem to have chickened out," Polly told him.

"Now, why would you want to do that?" Roger asked. "This is the perfect time of year for Paris."

"Roger," Polly bleated earnestly, "don't you think it's dangerous to go now?"

"Hell, no. Look, you're not flying TWA, right? Do you really think they're going to bother knocking off some dinky little charter?" He was the picture of stolid assurance.

"Well, but what about Paris itself?" Polly worried.

The waitress materialized at Roger's massive shoulder.

"Bring me a Jack Daniels and water, and another round of whatever the ladies were having."

I can't help it. An art critic who drinks Jack Daniels? At lunch? And he doesn't even have to bother arguing. Before my very eyes, he swept Polly's objections away with one dismissive wave of his big, beefy hand. "As a matter of fact, I have to be in London on the tenth. I don't see why I couldn't pop over and take you to dinner. How about it?" He pulled out a little engagement book. It looked ridiculous in his huge, hairy hand. "Where will you be staying?"

Polly didn't answer.

Miss Wiggy reappeared, and Roger beckoned largely, as though she was a fan far away in the stands of a stadium. "My daughter, Melissa," he explained, and as she came

nearer, I could see she was not a grown-up woman at all
—barely a teenager, in fact. I felt abruptly foolish in my
trendy getup. I stood. Roger, introducing us, picked up a
chair from a neighboring table.

"No, no, I was just going," I told him. Polly knows I
can't stand Roger. She gave me a look: pointed, yet difficult
to decipher. Reproach? Apology? Defiance? Getting up, I
noticed, as I have been noticing a lot lately, that I just can't
seem to drink like I used to. Of course, rage can cause
giddiness at any age.

"Roz?" Polly put her hand quietly on my arm. "Do you
happen to have the phone number of the Hotel Henri IV?"

See why I gave up sex?

TOOTH FAIRY

FOR QUENTIN CRISP

My name is Arthur. I'm Barbara's imaginary friend. And you, Reader, are *my* imaginary friend. How do *you* like it? I must say, I would find yours an intolerably marginal form of existence. My own is bad enough. But you're actually better off than I am. You can stop reading whenever you feel like it, after all. How would you like it if you were at my beck and call, had to talk and listen to me whenever I happened to be confused and lonely—and what if, like Barbara, I were always confused and lonely? Pity me, Reader. I can't call my soul my own, and I'm getting awfully tired of identifying with the likes of Prince Albert and Dennis Thatcher.

Of course, it is odd for an adult to have an imaginary friend. But then, Barbara is nothing if not odd. It is not for me to call my hostess insufferable, of course. And dependent on her as I am, it would scarcely be prudent. Let me tell you about her, though. Bear with me. In the end, you can judge for yourself.

She started having imaginary friends in her childhood. "Well," I seem to hear you ask, "what is so odd about that? Many children, especially only children, have imaginary friends." Of course they do. I myself (and I wasn't even an only child) had a teddy bear called Louie. I was a quiet boy, but Louie never seemed to shut up. I didn't mind, though. He was very good at putting things in perspective; he was loyal and affectionate; and late at night after everyone was asleep, he would sometimes transform himself into an eight-foot-tall pirate who beat and bound my elder sister and forced her to walk the plank. Once, when she had been particularly cruel to me, he went so far as to lash her to the mast and leave her for red ants to devour. Slowly.

But when she was the same age as I was when so humbly consoling myself with Louie, Barbara was talking to God. Don't get me wrong, Reader, I'm sure many people have talked and do talk to God in all humility, but not Barbara. To her, He was a kind of colleague. She took for granted His endorsement of her scorn for His creation. And the punishments He inflicted on her enemies made Louie's look harmless indeed. After all, even while the red ants were exposing my sister's skeletal structure, I knew she'd be there at the breakfast table, shoving porridge in my ear as likely as not. But what Barbara's God did to anyone who vexed her, He did for eternity. And what He did was not, as they say, pretty.

As she grew older, Barbara lost interest in God and felt no need of a new imaginary friend until the other day, when she brought me into being. God is a hard act to follow, believe me.

"I'm really stupid, aren't I, Arthur?" she asked me. "Only a stupid person could get herself into a situation like this, after all."

Now I could see that she wanted me to contradict her, tell her she was, despite appearances, some kind of genius.

But even a figment has some integrity, and while I don't believe she's as stupid as she says she is (and I don't even believe *she* thinks she's that stupid), I couldn't call her brilliant, either.

"Pride," I suggested. "That's your trouble. A bad habit to go carrying around from early childhood. Not for nothing is it the deadliest of the seven."

"Isn't that despair?"

I was no longer sure. "I don't know, but pride was what undid Lucifer. I wouldn't underestimate its deadliness if I were you."

"How do you mean?" she asked, but went on, without giving me a chance to explain, "You know, you're not what I thought you'd be like at all."

"Call the devil and he'll come," I said, and then I jumped because the thing I was sitting on started to emit an intolerably loud buzzing noise—like a bomber plane at very close range—while lurching and vibrating so that I was more or less launched off it. Staring back at it, I realized it was a washing machine.

"I'm sorry," she said. "It does that. I'm afraid it's on its last legs. I guess it must be awfully startling if you're not used to it."

"You know what I was doing before you brought me here to sit on your infernal machine?" I asked her furiously, once I regained my aplomb. "I was enjoying an excellent cassoulet in a charming restaurant. I was surrounded by attractive and stimulating companions. Dare one ask why you brought my lovely evening to such a premature and disagreeable end? I trust it was not simply to share the excitements of the Second Rinse Cycle?"

She had begun removing the laundry from the now quiescent machine. "For a good reason," she assured me, nodding glumly over the undershirts and towels.

"Things are really wrong, Arthur. Out-of-hand wrong. And I don't know if they always were, and I didn't know it, or whether they got that way because of things I did or didn't do, or whether there's any way I can *un*do them to get things back to a point that's, you know, reparable, or even whether I should if I could, if you know what I mean."

"If you expect me to know what you mean," I told her testily, "you should take the trouble to express yourself more clearly. 'Things are wrong,' you say. Could you be a bit more specific?"

"Please don't be so snippy!" she wailed. "I really need your help, that's what I made you up for, I need someone to help me think!"

"And that's just what I'm trying to do!" I pointed out.

"All right," she said, "what I mean is, I think my husband has gone crazy. But I don't know—maybe it's me. Or maybe it isn't that he's *gone* crazy, maybe he was crazy all along but I didn't realize it till recently. And then, there's craziness and craziness. I mean, he's entitled to be eccentric, isn't he? It's not like he's doing any harm to anyone but me, and even that's with my consent, really. I mean, I stay with him." At this point, Barbara started crying, with horrible gulping sobs. "Did I make him worse?" she howled. "Is it my fault for letting things get this bad?"

"You're getting tears on the laundry," I remarked.

"My God!" she hissed, sniffling. "I can't even *imagine* someone normal. Can't you see how miserable I am? How can you be so coldhearted? 'You're getting tears on the laundry.' " (She imitated my voice.) "Fat lot of help you are. Go away. I'm sorry I thought you up. Go on, scram, finish your cassoulet in peace."

"Madam," I told her stiffly, "I would like to point out that offering you a shoulder to saturate with your tears would not only be unconstructive but altogether out of character. I can see that you would like to be stroked and cuddled, and since you made me a homosexual, you should know that the idea of stroking and cuddling you is profoundly revolting to me—"

"That doesn't necessarily follow," she objected, still sniffing hideously. "Do you mind, about that? I mean, I couldn't have been comfortable, imagining a man to talk to who was, you know . . . I would feel disloyal. And I didn't want to talk to a woman somehow. Besides, I thought it would be fairer to my husband, to consult a masculine point of view."

I just stood there shaking my head. Really, I hardly knew where to begin on all that. Women! This creature pushes me into Sodom to satisfy her sense of propriety! Which of us is the pervert, I ask you?

"To return to the point," I said finally, "I could pat you on the head and say 'there, there' for an hour, and I would not have improved your situation at all. Nothing would have changed."

"Is that my problem?" she wondered forlornly. "Fear of change?"

I shook my head again. "Pride," I repeated. "But while we're on the subject, I would like to point out, just in case you hadn't noticed, that change is going to happen whatever you do, so you might as well commit yourself to getting the change you want, because if you don't . . ."

"Arthur?" she said. "Tell me one thing? Is he crazy?"

"Yes."

She stared at me till her tears started flowing again.

"That isn't really what you brought me here to tell you, is it?" I asked her. "You know quite well he's crazy. What you want to know is what to do about it."

"Do I have a right to do anything? I mean, oh dear, oh dear, oh dear." The woman began sobbing helplessly, like a very small child.

"Pull yourself together, damn it," I said. "Go wash your face. Comb your hair."

"Listen," she urged me hoarsely, "he's dragging me under with him. Look at me!"

"I'd rather not," I said coldly. "It's a most unattractive spectacle."

"Look, I'm his *wife*. You'd think I could force him to go to a psychiatrist or something, but in the first place he doesn't believe in psychiatrists, and in the second place *I* don't believe in psychiatrists. It's not like he's doing anything antisocial enough to be locked up for. Or even to make him into an emergency, at least not to anyone but me. Besides, besides . . . psychiatrists don't change anyone's behavior. I've known lots of people who went to psychiatrists, and if it changed them at all, it only made them more neurotic. What it is, I think, is that they lose all sense of shame.

"And anyway, even if I believed it would do him any good to see a psychiatrist, and even if we could pay for it, I couldn't get him to go! Look at his teeth!"

"Must I?"

"God!" she cried. "I must deserve my misery. I'm the most ineffectual person I ever heard of! I try to invoke the Voice of Reason, and all I can come up with is some sarcastic old queen. You're no help at all, you know."

"Sticks and stones will break my bones . . ." I muttered. "What about his teeth, then?"

"Look at me!" She dropped the laundry and shook her hands wildly and pointlessly in my face. "Do you know how much I weigh? Do you know why? The man has an irrational fear of dentists. He hasn't been to a dentist since he was sixteen years old!

"And he gets these toothaches, and he goes wild, from incredibly bad-tempered to outright violent, and I mean, I've done everything I could think of to persuade him to go, but after all, I can't get the cops to come after him and put him in handcuffs and drag him to a dentist, can I? He has a perfect right not to go, even if the pain does make him into such a beast that he doesn't know what he's doing. And how can anyone judge how bad someone else's toothache is? It's the most subjective thing there is, pain.

"But if all that is true for me about him, it's true for him about me, too. See, he's not just afraid of dentists for himself. He believes—sincerely believes—they're evil. So he won't let me go, either. He claims every woman he's ever known has had at least one dentist make a pass at her right there on the chair, which I wouldn't think was a very erotic situation, but he swears it happened, even to his mother. So I said I'd go to a woman dentist, and he said, 'You'd trust a woman to take care of your teeth?' But there aren't any female dentists around here anyway.

"Now my teeth are giving out. Look at me, Arthur! Not one bite has crossed my lips since this abscess. I think it must be an abscess. It's nearly five weeks now. It didn't start out as a hunger strike; I didn't eat, in the beginning, because I couldn't—it hurt too much. And then I got the idea of *using* that, the not eating. I thought surely it would melt his heart to see me getting thinner and thinner, and he'd overcome his fear for my sake and we'd both go to the dentist and everything would be all right. So I told him I wouldn't eat until I'd been to a dentist, and I wouldn't go to a dentist till he did. You'd think a man would care, wouldn't you, if his wife was starving herself to death? It's been a month since I said that. He's stubborn.

"Isn't it sad? I always wanted a figure like this. And now that I've got it, I'm too miserable to enjoy it. I measured my waist yesterday. Twenty-one inches! Look!" She grabbed the waistband of her skirt and held it far away from her body. "My clothes are falling off! And I don't even have the energy to alter them. How long can a person live on broth and fruit juice?

"And it's making me crazy, too. It's all very well for you to be supercilious—I'd just like to know if you could think straight in my situation—"

"I *never* think straight," I interrupted.

She went on as if I hadn't spoken. "I don't know if it's the pain itself, or the fasting—I must have all kinds of deficiencies by now, vitamins and proteins, and doesn't that interfere with your ability to think clearly? I'm sure it does—or the painkillers I've been taking, maybe they make me confused. They're just over-the-counter stuff, but I could have paid a dentist twice by now with all I've spent on these pills, not to mention with what I've saved on food, but I can't cope if I don't take them, the pain is too bad;

I can't get even the simplest chores done, I just cry all the time. Oh dear, oh dear. I seem to be crying all the time even if I do take them.

"Help me, Arthur, dammit! Can't you see I've lost it? I don't know what I'm doing! I'll die if this goes on! I can't think anymore! Tell me what to do!"

"I told you what to do. Wash your face. Comb your hair."

"Oh, God! Is that the best you can come up with? So I'll be a neat and tidy corpse—great. Swell. Wonderful. You've been enormously helpful, how can I ever thank you enough?"

"I'm not sure I blame your husband for hitting you," I told her. "If you can tell me how a messy corpse is superior to a tidy one, I'll apologize. If and only if.

"I repeat: Wash your face and comb your hair. *Then*, get your purse, put on your coat and boots, and walk out the door. Don't stop till you get to your neighbor's. Ask her to take you to a hospital."

"Oh, Arthur," she said, abruptly tearless. "I couldn't do that. I'm not sick enough for a hospital, am I? I mean, it's nothing that couldn't be fixed by having the tooth out and eating a meal or two."

"Make up your mind," I said. "A moment ago you were dying."

"No one ever died of a toothache," she said. "Did they?"

I didn't answer.

"People got along for centuries and centuries without dentists; of course, they died in droves from things like puerperal fever and bubonic plague, but not toothache, did they? Won't it just fall out eventually? If I can wait it out, I mean?

"And you know, it would be the end—of my marriage, I mean—if I did anything like what you're telling me to do. He'd never forgive me. And you know something, Arthur? Even if he did forgive me, I don't think I could bring myself to go back to him, once I experienced some other kind of life. By now, I'm sort of used to this crazy isolation—one house after another, always out in the country, miles from nowhere with no car, never staying in one place long enough to know the neighbors.

"I can't even remember what it was like, before I got married. It's almost ten years. I know—in a way—there's a world out there where it would be possible to lead a calm, normal, reasonable sort of life, but it's been so long since I've experienced anything like that . . . all this time, he's been my whole world. Oh, Arthur, if I got a real taste of another kind of life, I couldn't go back."

"Tell me," I asked her, "did you bring me here to persuade you to leave him, or to persuade you to stay?"

"I don't know," she said. "I think—I'm afraid—I don't know how to put this, but I've lost all sense of him as a human being. It's not a matter of leaving *him* or not leaving *him*, it's leaving *marriage*. It doesn't make sense, does it? I mean, what I can't bear the thought of doing is breaking my promise. Marriage is an absolute commitment, isn't it? Better, worse, sickness, health. Those are the terms, aren't they? There wouldn't be any point in marriage if sickness lets you off the hook, would there?"

"What century are you living in, my dear?" I asked. "It's been quite some time since marriage was viewed so absolutely, especially in the society you were born into. I told you your trouble was pride. If it wasn't for your pride, you would have left him on your honeymoon. Hoity-toity! You found you'd married a nut, and told yourself you'd found a man with a truly independent mind, didn't you?

"You make me sick, frankly. The self-importance! The fate of Western civilization hangs on the question of your going to a dentist! *Listen* to yourself."

"You creep! I'm in *pain*," she yammered, "and maybe it's not very important about me in particular, but it's an important question, whether marriage is or is not absolute."

"Not to me," I muttered.

"I'm not thinking clearly," she groaned. "I'd like to

see you thinking clearly with a raging toothache, not having eaten for more than a month! You dare talk to me about my pride! It's all very well for you, you supercilious pederast, you don't understand at all, what do you know? You're no good to me. I don't know why I thought you up. Scram! Unbe! Go back to your damned dinner party."

And I did, but she kept bringing me back. I won't burden you with the conversations we had; they were all similar to the first one. She was always in tears, and each time a little wilder and a little bonier. Can you imagine what my life was like? One moment I'd be sitting in my office, cracking open rolls of quarters on the side of my desk, or riding a bus, missing my stop in fact because I was reading Poe's "Berenice," and I'd find myself, without warning, sitting in her filthy depressing kitchen. Twice, she even dragged me away from the theater (the second act of *Little Shop of Horrors* and the first act of *You Never Can Tell*) to listen to her pointless whining.

I never saw her husband. I began to find myself sympathizing with him, though. This woman, I felt, would drive anyone mad.

One day she said, "He's no realer than you are, really. When you come right down to it, everyone we know is a figment of our imaginations. We think about what we hear them say and see them do, and we sort of construct a personality on the basis of what we think they're like from all that. Is that any more real than outright invention, from scratch?"

I was exasperated. My life is a selfish one, I admit, but I harm no one. I cannot see what right this woman has to bore me with her infantile speculations and her circular arguments whenever she wants a listening ear, no matter what I may happen to be doing at the time.

"Very well," I said, "perhaps it is you who are mad, perhaps your husband is perfectly sane. If you are the mad one, wouldn't the best thing you could do be to kill yourself? You're miserable. And you certainly aren't doing your

husband any good. Why not put an end to it? Kill yourself?"

"I'm not completely useless," she protested after staring
at me for a while. "I cook for him at least. I do his laundry,
his mending. I keep the house clean."

"Not very," I told her. "Besides, it's not as if we were
talking about specialized skills. He can find someone else
to do those things for him, don't you think?"

"There can't be two such fools in this world," she mumbled, starting, as usual, to cry. "Oh dear, oh dear, this is
intolerable."

"You're telling me!" I snapped. "Look, I'm not asking
you to do anything you aren't doing anyway. All I'm saying is, why prolong it? You're killing yourself slowly, what
else do you think you're doing, I'd like to know? It's been
two months since you started this so-called hunger strike.
Surely you can't delude yourself that it could have any
constructive results? How is your husband, hmmmm?"

"Worse," she said. "Worse and worse every day."

"Very well," I said. "There are three things you can
do. One: Stay with him as you are, with both of you getting
worse every day, until one of you dies or does something
mad enough to attract society's attention. So far as I can
see, nothing is to be gained from that approach. You will
have the satisfaction of dying with a clear conscience, of
course, knowing that you haven't broken any promises,
but I don't see what good that does anyone. So. That brings
us to Two. Go. Do whatever you have to do to get your
teeth fixed, and if the pain and the starving are what have
driven you wild, perhaps you'll be able to think clearly
once you're physically all right. Although knowing you,
I'm inclined to doubt it. Three: Kill yourself. That way
you can at least be certain of putting two people out of
their misery."

"But maybe he needs me. I know he's miserable now,
but maybe he'd be even more miserable if I was dead," she
blubbered.

"It was *my* misery I was thinking of. You can't suppose I enjoy listening to your troubles?"

"I didn't create you for your own enjoyment!" she bellowed. "I thought you would *help*. No wonder you want to kill yourself, you're even more useless than I am."

"Who said I wanted to kill myself?" I asked her. "We were talking about *you* killing yourself."

"Can't have one without the other, Arthur. You exist in my consciousness. Without that, there'd be no you."

I hadn't thought of that before. "It's a mysterious thing, existence," I told her, hedging, feeling nonplussed. "I seem to remember a life that has nothing to do with you— memories of my childhood, my teddy bear, my sister, years and years before I ever saw your wretched kitchen or heard your whining voice. It's hard to believe that if you died, it would all never have existed."

She snorted. "I wouldn't even have to die," she said. "All I'd have to do is never think about you again. That life of yours you're always telling me I'm interrupting— you take it for granted, but where do you think it comes from, anyway? I imagine it, that's where it comes from. God, you're ungrateful."

I couldn't think of anything to say.

"You know, Arthur," she went on. "I haven't been enjoying your company any more than you've been enjoying mine. How does Cole Porter put it? 'It's been great fun, but it was just one of those things'?"

"Don't do anything rash," I begged her. A life at Barbara's beck and call was far from enjoyable, certainly, but it did seem better than no life at all.

"No one has the courage of their convictions," she sneered. "A moment ago you were urging me to kill myself. Why should I let you live? You're a parasite! What good are you? I thought it would help if I had someone to talk to. I was wrong. I should have made you a dentist. That would have been more to the point."

"I suppose I could learn dentistry," I heard myself say.

"I suppose you could," she said. And she smiled. It

was a horrible sight. I realized it was the first time I'd ever
seen her smile, in all those weeks.

"What are you doing?" I asked her as she began to
rummage in a drawer.

She fished out a pair of pliers. She brandished them—
there's no other word for it—in my face. "Pull it," she
commanded.

"I can't pull teeth!" I told her. "Really, I wouldn't
know what I was doing. It would get infected or something.
You'd be worse off than ever. Really, I couldn't go through
with it anyway. I never could stand the sight of blood.
Please put those things away. You don't know what you're
asking."

"Oh, come on, Arthur. You can do it. You can't fool
me. I know all about your sadistic fantasies about your
sister. Oh, why didn't I think of this before? It's just that
I couldn't stand the thought of doing it myself, it's too
unnerving. Besides, it's already quite loose. One good yank
should do it. Don't tell me you can't manage that."

I backed away from her, shaking my head.

"If that's a final refusal," she told me, tapping the pliers
on the edge of the kitchen table, "I guess I'll just have to
replace you with someone more cooperative." Keeping up
the percussive effect of the pliers, she began to hum "Just
One of Those Things."

Of course, I did it. If I hadn't, I'd be in no position to
tell you all this, would I? But I did not leave the customary
quarter under her pillow. Even a figment is entitled to draw
the line somewhere. I haven't seen her since that day, but
as my life goes on, I know she's still thinking about me.
And I, miserably, still think of her. For one thing, I live
in fear of the day it occurs to her to bring me back to take
the pliers to that husband of hers.

AFTER THE BALL

FOR JONATHAN CANNO

Tonight, I'm going to my cousin Charlotte's coming-out party. I know I'm going to have a lousy time—I always do, at parties. Academically, I'm hot stuff, but socially, forget it. But although I never expected to enjoy myself, I'd been horrified at the thought that I might not be allowed to go to this party. My mother had said, at first, that I was too young.

I whined, wheedled, and argued. My sixteen-year-old cousin Dabney was going—a junior in high school. A year ahead of myself, I, too, am a junior in high school. Which is why, later in the winter, I'll be going to the same predeb parties as Dabney. So, I said, if Dabney could go to Charlotte's ball, why couldn't I? And in the end, I got my way.

So I'm extra-sulky this morning, dawdling over my breakfast, brooding over the Pyrrhic nature of my victory. I'm trying to enjoy the thought of wearing a long grown-up evening dress, since I figure that's the only pleasure the party's going to offer me. I'm also procrastinating getting up from the table because the next event on my agenda is a trip to the hairdresser's, where I'm going to have to spend the entire day. My hair is ridiculously thick, and nearly reaches my knees. Once wound over rollers, it takes the better part of a day to dry. Trying to look on the bright side, I tell myself I can read *Anna Karenina* from cover to cover under the drier, which is what I plan to do.

I figure the ball is going to be just like school dances, but with more people. What I hate about school dances is the boys. There are two kinds: too tall, and too short. The tall ones hunch over me and step on my feet while I try to make conversation with their rib cages. I hunch over the short ones and I step on their feet while I aim questions down at the tops of their heads.

I am not good at talking to boys. I know what I am supposed to do: Be a good listener, draw them out. But it is hard for me even to want to do these things. Besides, I talk too fast.

I get up from the table to hone my social skills for a while before leaving the dining room. Cherubino, my mother's toy poodle, who has been lurking under the table in case of crumbs, follows me, not very hopefully. I face the mirror over the sideboard, simpering politely. I ask my reflection "Do you like sports?" It doesn't; it sticks out its tongue. I try again. I *will* remember not to talk too fast. "Do (pause-two-three-four) you (pause-two-three-four) like . . ." Much too slow. And awfully unnatural. "Do (Young Lochin—) you (var has come) like (out of the) sports?" *Much* better. "What (The Assyr—) school (ian came down) do (like a wolf)—"

Behind my reflection in the mirror, my mother's appears in the doorway at the far end of the room. Her beautiful face depresses me. It isn't just that I know I'll never be beautiful; there's something authentically creepy in its perfection. My friends always say she looks like the Wicked Queen in Walt Disney's movie of Snow White. Yes, widow's peak and all, the cartoon could be a caricature of her, but the essence of the resemblance is: Her makeup never smears or fades; her nail polish never chips; her stockings never run.

"I wish I were happier about that dress," she says, without so much as a good morning.

I am wearing a bathrobe. When it was hers, it was a peignoir; now that it is mine, it is a bathrobe. She means the dress I am going to wear to the ball.

"It's a beautiful dress," I tell her, suddenly afraid she'll take it away somehow, when wearing it is going to be the only nice thing that's going to happen to me all night. "And it would be such a waste not to wear it, after getting the shoes made and everything."

Like my robe, the dress used to be hers. When she bought it, it had, just where the train started in back, a rather pointless bow. This bow her dressmaker removed, using some of the fabric to put little panels under the armholes, to accommodate my bust. The rest of the fabric was used to cover a pair of shoes.

My mother glides up behind me, pulls back the robe. Like a window dresser with a size-twelve dress to display on a size-six mannequin, she tugs, puffs, stretches, and bunches until the facade of the shapeless robe has taken on the contours of the empire-waisted evening dress. In case I have missed the point, she explains: "The bow balanced your bosom."

I hate this subject, but my mother won't let it alone. These days it seems she cannot catch sight of me without disparaging my figure, which consists only of my bust: The rest of me is still a bony little girl. Almost automatically —it is only a year or two since I have done this by the hour, playing jacks—I mutter, "The big blue bow balanced baby's bulging—"

With a quick, outbreathed snort, she drops the parts of the robe she has been holding. She is, all at once, gone. Cherubino scrambles after her. Smoothing my robe back into shapelessness, I listen until I can no longer hear the slap of her heels against her slippers.

I turn back to the mirror, but I have no more heart for conversation practice. What's the use? I'm going to have a lousy time; the boys will be sniggering at my unbalanced bosom. I don't care. I don't like boys anyway. Not that I know much about them. I have no brothers; I've spent my life in girls' schools. I have formed my impressions of boys, though. They are ugly, they are noisy, they are violent, and above all they are boring. They are interested in one thing only, and that thing is sports.

Of course, I have read about boys who are not like this. But then, I have also read about centaurs, werewolves, and mermaids, and I don't expect to find any of those at my cousin Charlotte's coming-out party, either.

I head back to my room, to use the remaining minutes before I have to dress for the hairdresser to rip out a few inches of the hem of the train of my evening dress. Into the pocket I've formed, I thrust *Les Fleurs du Mal*. Not really what I would have chosen for the occasion, but the only book I can find that's small enough to fit. Then I pin the hem back up with safety pins. This way, if the ball is as bad as I think it's going to be, I can hide in the ladies' room reading Baudelaire until the party's over.

By the time I'm wearing the dress, with the light weight of the book occasionally discernible against my ankles, I'm a different person, externally. I think I'm the same as ever inside, but I can't be sure. My hair, irrepressible for as long as I can remember—shedding barrettes, escaping from braids—has been compressed into fat, improbable ringlets that bounce along my neck like Slinky Toys. What has happened to my face is even more amazing. It has been transformed twice. My mother didn't like it the first time. I sat in the makeup artist's little room, marveling at what I saw in the mirror: not my podgy, pale face but a ballerina's, all eyes. My mother came in to inspect its progress. "*False eyelashes?*" she asked the makeup artist, reaching into my face to rip one off with her long red nails, fresh from the manicurist. "On a child of fifteen? What can you be thinking of?"

Tears came into my half-denuded eyes. She was spoiling my brand-new grown-up face, and besides I was horrified that she could speak so disrespectfully to the makeup artist. He was *famous*. Under the drier, I had become exasperated with Anna—leaving a perfectly good family for a short-haired soldier (yecch!)—and begun to leaf through *Vogue*, and there he was, being interviewed, the very same man who was about to do my face. Yet my mother didn't faze him: Calmly, he removed the ballerina with cleansing cream and started over.

She was right. How do grown-ups know these things? The second face is much better than the first. My mother would no more have considered sending me to a ball without makeup than without clothes, but it had to look natural. No, that wasn't it: Nature could never have produced what I saw in the mirror, though the colors on my face ("sable," "tea rose," "aquamarine") were named for animals, vegetables, and minerals. I decided it had to look as if it was *trying* to look natural.

I'm already tired. I want to go home. But I am home —we haven't left yet. I'm almost angry, now, that I have a ball to go to: This strange soubrette in the mirror is giving me quite enough to think about.

My father's at the door of my room, resplendent in white tie. He's grinning at the sight of me. He's a yanker of braids, a tousler of bangs: I put my hands up to guard my new hair as he comes toward me. "Don't mess it up," I beg.

"May I kiss your hand, Madame?" he asks.

I extend it. I think he's being silly, but I am also deeply pleased that something about the way I now look has stopped him from pulling my hair.

On his way out, though, he tweaks one of the ringlets after all. "Couldn't resist," he says, with his mischievous smile. He takes for granted that this smile will get him forgiven for everything by everybody, because usually it

does. He's "boyish," everyone says. So what has he got
to teach me? When I am grown up, the opposite sex is
going to consist not of boys but of men. I think of this
sometimes. It comforts me.

My male cousins dance with me, at the ball, I think because their mothers insist on it. My mother was one of eight
children, so on her side of the family, which is the one my
cousin Charlotte comes from, there's a steady supply of
partners for me. I already know whether they like sports, and
which ones, and even what positions they play, but they bring
friends and roommates to dance with me too, so I have a
chance to practice slow conversation after all. There's something I don't like about seeing all these boys and men in evening dress. They seem reduced to some painfully common
denominator that way, like soldiers in uniform.

An aunt introduces me to a man with a name I admire.
"Did you know," I ask him, "that there's a man with your
name who translated Alphonse Daudet and—"

"The sins of my youth," he says.

"You mean it was *you*?" I ask, astonished.

He smiles, nods, somehow coyly.

This is unthinkable, almost unbearable. I stare and stare
at him. So far as I have ever known, the things that are
important to my parents and the things that are important
to me are two worlds as distinct as Saturn and Mars. This
party is an event in my parents' world. Reading Daudet is
an event in mine. Tentatively, I have been forming a plan:
I will simply never leave school—I will stay as long as I
can as a student, and after that, I will stay as a teacher. In
this way, I will never have to enter—and fail in—my parents' world. But now it seems that's no good after all. Here
is this man who's translated Daudet, and it hasn't saved
him from having to sashay around this ballroom in white
tie, being polite to my aunts.

My cousin Joe, one of my horsey, Southern cousins,
comes lurching toward me with another, very ugly boy.
"My roommate," he drawls. "I thought you-all might have
something in common."

This does not seem likely to me, and judging from the way Joe's roommate is looking at me, it seems even less likely to him. I can't help respecting the way he sneers. I wish I had his nerve, but I don't. To make up for my defects, I'm as eager to please as a puppy. And then this roommate has hardly started fox-trotting with me when we discover we like all the same writers. I mean, Evelyn Waugh is one thing, but Max Beerbohm! I didn't think anyone in the world except my English teacher had ever even *heard* of Max Beerbohm.

Although I've been making no effort to speak to him slowly, there isn't time for much of our thrilling mutual discovery. Henry Alcott is cutting in. I have nothing against Henry, tallest of all the ridiculously tall Alcott boys whose parents' summer house is down the road from my parents' summer house, but it seems hard to be snatched so soon from my soul mate. Will I ever see him again? I haven't even heard his name. By the time the fox-trot ends, I've spotted him way on the other side of the dance floor with my cousin Dabney.

No time to think about him now; the band has launched into a full-fledged exuberant waltz—I've never heard Strauss played so fast—and Henry is whirling me high, high, higher and faster than I've ever whirled before. Henry's six foot seven: He's holding me tight, my feet aren't touching the floor at all, or only brushing it in passing. For a moment, I remember exactly what it was like to be an infant, delighted to be picked up and swung, way up there, by an enormous, infallibly reliable grown-up. But this is better. I have never suspected that anything physical could be so exhilarating. It is like being an angel hurtling through the sky in a ceiling painted by Tiepolo. From time to time the flowers of evil slap gently at my heels. I have forgotten about the book in my hem. I notice, but cannot account for, the sensation.

When the music stops, Henry and I are next to my father and a woman called Mrs. Wheeler, whom my parents are being nice to because her husband left her very suddenly. I feel sorry for Mrs. Wheeler, especially now when I'm so giddily ecstatic. I like her: She is kind and funny; how could anyone leave her? But I can't pity her now. She has been transformed, as I have; her hair, which usually starts in graying, mousy roots, and straggles down her face in brassy strings, is smooth, and a pale, even gold all over. She doesn't look sad. She is leaning on my father with one hand, tightening the strap of a gold sandal with the other. My father and she are both laughing, looking down at her foot. I would prefer it if she was sad, so that I could feel sorry for her. I am so relieved at the way boys are turning out to be. I need release from this relief; I want to be magnanimous.

A waiter appears at her side with a tray: glasses of champagne. I'm awfully thirsty, after all that dancing, but I have been strictly forbidden to have more than two glasses, and the fact is, I've already had three. Does my father know? But he is handing me a glass from the tray.

Miracle succeeds miracle. By the time I'm allowed to go on to a club with some of the others, I'm perversely resentful. Why is my mother letting me do this? Does she mean to stop taking care of me?

By the time Henry brings me home, I am utterly caught up in planning what I will say to my mother. I want to burst in on her in bed. I don't enjoy talking to her, but there's so much I need to tell her. As I see it, she has wronged me. All these years, she has been teaching me about a world where I will be unwelcome, and, after all, it's a world that doesn't exist. Why, if I hadn't gone to this party—and she didn't want me to go, at first—I might have spent the rest of my life in school, hiding.

I picture myself standing in her room, denouncing her, itemizing my social triumphs as she cowers in her vast bed. ("Did you see, Mummy? Did you see how many boys danced with me? Did you see how long Mr. Prendergast talked to me? He's *famous*, you know. Did you see how I made him laugh?") Thinking about talking to my mother, I can scarcely pay attention to Henry's trying to kiss me. Absentmindedly, I duck under his arms with a step I have learned in Morris dancing and shut the front door on him. Then I wonder, What have I done? Passed up my first kiss!

I see that as my mother's fault, too.

And then it turns out I can't barge into her room to confront her: She is not there. I hear her voice—lots of voices—in the dining room. I can smell coffee, bacon. I'm hungry, but how can I bear eating breakfast, being polite to a bunch of grown-ups instead of telling my mother what's on my mind. I stay in the living room, irresolute.

This room is not itself. My father, evidently, paid the band to come home with him. It's a thing he does sometimes. My mother doesn't like it, but he hates parties to be over. The carpet is rolled up at one edge of the room, the furniture is pushed against the walls, there are glasses and ashtrays everywhere making garbage-y, grown-up smells. It's defeating, somehow.

By the time my mother discovers me slumped, dozing in a corner of the sofa, I've lost my impetus. But I try to work it up again. "Did you see, Mummy? I was so *popular.*"

"Jews," says my mother, "and pansies." Normally, as she knows, either of these words will send me into raging speeches that end in slammed doors and tears.

"I see how it's going to be, with you," she adds.

I straighten up on the sofa and stare at her, but although I open my mouth, nothing comes out.

My mother is holding a piece of bacon between two red-clawed fingers. Cherubino leaps for it, yipping. She raises it higher. He leaps higher, falls, his little legs bend under him in a painful-looking tangle.

She no longer matters. I'm exhilarated, gleeful, intoxicated, knowing this. And I'm staggered. My joy frightens me, makes me guilty, but I can't unfeel it, can't persuade myself to enter the fight she's trying to pick. I'm even sorry for her—still trying to fight, when she's already beaten. No wonder she hates to see me getting a figure. My growing up is her growing old.

* * *

Ten years later, I will tell this story, the story of my first ball, to my stepdaughter Lolly. She will be fifteen, about to go to her first school dance.

I will have been committed to avoiding my mother's mistakes. I will never have said anything to make Lolly self-conscious about her enormous bottom. The sight of her, in the tight jeans she will favor, will be painful to me; I will reproach myself for minding (it's trivial); I will strive to purge myself of my mother's values.

So Lolly will head off for the dance in tight jeans, with a short jacket over a tight sweater, and hideous, clumsy Dr. Martin boots—an outfit so unbecoming that it will seem to me to have been assembled from a fear of social failure so strong as to prevent Lolly from trying at all. I will have given Lolly an option; I will have made her a dress. I will have adapted the pattern to her needs; I will have spent the week's food money on fabric with enough body not to droop where I gather it in front to create the illusion of a chest. But Lolly will not avail herself of this option.

When I tell her the story of my first ball, I will censor it. I will not tell her exactly what my mother said, the next morning; I will have her say, instead of "Jews and pansies," "intellectuals," which, in fact, she did say, on other, later occasions. Censoring will make me uneasy: We owe our children protection, but we owe them the truth, too—in fact, we owe them the truth precisely because it can provide protection for them.

I will not tell Lolly how happy it made me to realize that I would be alive—and in my prime—when my mother was dead.

I will tell her nothing but the ugly-duckling story: I will want it to comfort her, I will want it to give her hope, because Lolly, at fifteen, will be so very unattractive. After all, it cheered me so much just to suspect that I could be liked without being beautiful.

But Lolly will say, "It's like—another century, you know?"

* * *

When Lolly comes home from the dance, I will see from her face how it was. I will ache for her, remembering the intensity of a fifteen-year-old's feelings, seeing how hard she is pretending not to mind. And I will know her feelings to be more intense than mine were at her age.

"School dances!" I'll say, brightly. "What did I tell you?" Meaning her to believe her day, her ball, her waltz, her prince will come.

But they will never come in any form I know how to recognize. She will be such a bitter, angry, lonely feminist —by the time she is thirty and I am forty, we will have nothing to say to each other, although we will never stop trying to talk.

And by that time I will have begun to hear myself using my mother's voice, my mother's words. Not all of them. In a single hour, I will hear myself say, "But what can you expect, hanging out with yuppies?" just as she would ask me what I could expect, going out with Jews; then, "Avoid him, dear—pure Eurotrash" (and I will fill in that blank easily); and then I will call my secretary, "Edgar DAMMIT, I need you," as I heard her, a thousand thousand times, call her maid.

My stockings will never run (I will always carry two extra pairs). My nail polish will never chip (I will always carry a spare bottle of the right color). I will spot her gestures in mirrors until they no longer startle me.

But in 1963, I don't know that any of this is going to happen. I stand next to my mother at the window, looking out, and I marvel at the size of the city I live in. It occurs to me that I have never been west of the park by myself. And then I decide that my mother has probably never been west of the park by herself, and for that reason, I change my clothes and go out, heading west, fearless and happy. Because I believe that when she is dead, she will be gone.

CORPORAL PUNISHMENT

FOR SIGMUND FLOYD

"**Y**ou mean," Max snorted, banging his fist on the table so that the dishes and glasses and silverware jumped and lurched, "that some English creep is allowed to pull up the girls' skirts and hit them? Huh? Lolly, is that what you are telling me?"

I looked at Lolly, his daughter. When Max was angry, I could hardly bear to look at him; I felt as if I had turned to liquid in my terror. He might do anything, break all the rules—one reason I had married him.

I wanted to cover Lolly's ears and eyes: Where I came from, little girls were not exposed to outbursts like that. But I also wanted to learn about Max from Lolly, who had known him for all ten years of her life. I'd only been married for seven months.

Lolly was scared, too, backing down fast. "Oh, no," she said, "I think it's just the boys who get caned. I mean, I don't even know about that. I never heard of anyone hitting a girl, really. I don't even know if it's true about the boys. Maybe they were just, you know, saying it . . ." Lolly was twisting her right thumb in her left fist on her lap, something she does when she's worried.

"Corporal punishment for children!" Max exploded. "In 1968! Goddamn barbarians," he huffed. "This country that thinks it's so *civilized*." He looked at me, meaningfully. Somehow, I had become responsible for all of England's sins. I'm not English, and I'd never been to England before, but although Max had lived in London for nearly two years altogether, at different times, I knew much more about the country than he did. I had studied English history and English literature, and I had several English friends. When I tried to share my knowledge with him, he would often mistake description for advocacy. "Lolly, if anybody ever *talks* about touching you, anything, you just walk right out the door of Richmond Secondary Modern— *Modern!*—School and come straight home. And you'll never go back."

Lolly nodded, still twisting her thumb in her fist, not looking up at him. But she said, "Did they used to hit kids when you were at school, back in the olden days?" So his rage couldn't be as awful as it seemed, because Lolly knew quite well how sensitive Max had become about his age since marrying me, and here she was teasing him.

When would I know Max as well as Lolly did? Pleasantly enough, Max said, "Oh, yes. I went to terrible schools, you know. Back in the Dark Ages." Lolly certainly knew what she was doing. "My third-grade teacher, Miss MacFarquahar, she used to make me march up to her desk and stick out my hands, and she'd hit me on the knuckles with her ruler. I *still* have nightmares about Miss Mac-Farquahar and her ruler. Especially because it was *my hands*." Max put down his knife and fork (Lolly and I hadn't picked ours up since he banged his fist on the table) and stared tenderly at the paint under his fingernails. He looked from me to Lolly, his enormous dark eyes inviting us girls to feel sorry for the little boy he had once been. "Of course,

I didn't know I was going to be a painter, but I was drawing all the time. It wasn't just the pain, you see. I'd be afraid she was going to hurt my fingers so I couldn't move them, couldn't draw anymore. I kept having this dream, where she'd hit me and my hands would be all swollen up and stiff . . ." Max seemed lost in remembering the horror of his dream.

"But did she really hurt you? In real life?" I wanted to know.

"It stung," Max told me. "It was the psychological pain that was worst, though."

"What's psychological?" Lolly asked.

"In your mind," Max explained.

"*I'd* rather have pain in my mind," said Lolly indistinctly.

"Don't talk with your mouth full, darling," I reminded her.

"I wish you would stop calling Lolly 'darling,' " Max said. "You sound like your mother, for Christ's sake."

I was about to defend myself, having said "darling" to make sure Lolly would know she was only being reminded, not scolded, when I saw Max's point. The children at Richmond Secondary Modern School were *tough*. I had an agonized vision of Lolly being tortured on a muddy playground for some la-di-da trick of speech.

"Did they do capital punishment to *you*?" Lolly asked me.

I had just taken a sip of water, and I choked on my laughter, and Max, also laughing, got up to thump me on the back.

"Don't laugh with your mouth full, *darling*," Lolly advised me smugly, giggling.

When I could breathe again, Max said, "*Corporal* punishment, Lolly. *Capital* punishment means killing people."

"Kids?" Lolly asked dubiously.

"No, no," Max assured her. "Grown-ups. If they've done something like murder."

"Tonight," said Lolly, "I want a bedtime story about corporal punishment."

Lolly clung, at ten, to the privilege of bedtime stories. Max had worn through his repertoire by the time I entered the family: Lolly was delighted when she found I knew so many stories she had never heard before. I was pleased, too. For one thing, I was worried about Lolly's education. When we'd arrived in England, we were just too late for Lolly to take the eleven-plus exams, which were over for that spring. Since she knew neither French nor Latin, she wouldn't have had much of a chance anyway, but we were told she could sit for them in the fall if she could be prepared. I told Max I thought I could cram her in French and Latin over the summer.

"French and Latin," Lolly had said. "Yukky. I don't want to. Why do I have to learn French and Latin?"

"You don't," Max had said firmly.

"But, Max, I really think Lolly should be in a grammar school. A secondary modern is like—like a vocational school or something, in America. I mean, she couldn't go on to college."

"I'm not sure I want her to go to college, and I'm not sure we'll still be in England in the fall," Max had said.

"But just in case we *are* still in England?" I had suggested. "It certainly won't do her any harm, learning a little French and Latin."

"It's not as if Lolly were a boy," Max had said. "Teach her to cook. What good have French and Latin done *you*?"

"Lifetime supply of bedtime stories," was the best answer I could think to make.

It was edging into winter, and we were still in England. Max's London gallery hadn't sold one of his paintings since the spring, so we had no prospect of leaving. Max painted desperately, all day, every day. The only thing Lolly seemed to be learning in school was working-class diction. Alone with her, feeding her a snack after school or telling her stories at night, I was relentlessly informative, but I sometimes asked myself why. Did I want Lolly to grow up like me: all dressed up, mentally, with no place to go?

That night, Lolly reminded me, "A story about corporal punishment."

I didn't need reminding. I had been working it out while doing the dinner dishes.

"First, Lolly, let me tell you where this story comes from."

"I don't *care* where it comes from. That's boring. Why do you always have to talk about that? I just want to hear the story."

She made flapping, impatient gestures with her arms, and her shabby, threadbare nightgown ripped about four inches down the back.

"Take it off, Lol, I'll mend it while I tell you the story."

"Can't you do it tomorrow? It's so cold."

"All right," I told her, but as I looked at the rip, I thought the cloth was really too rotten for mending. Max and I had come to a deadlock on the issue of Lolly's need for new clothes. I thought we should buy a few things secondhand to tide her over till he sold another painting. To Max, the purchase would mean I didn't believe he was going to sell another painting in the immediate future. So Lolly went around with a three-inch gap between the ends of her coat sleeves (let down as far as they would go) and the tops of her mittens (which I had made for her out of an old pair of Max's socks).

"It's a cold story," I told her. "Think about Russia, remember when you went through the U.S.S.R. on a train with Daddy?"

"It wasn't cold," Lolly said. "It was summer."

"Yes, but in this story, it's winter. Think of that flat land, going on and on out the windows of the train, but it's all covered with snow, and the snow is still falling. The czar is in his palace in Petrograd—that's Leningrad, now; you were there, remember?"

"I thought the star was on the train," said Lolly.

"The czar."

"What's the czar?"

"*What* do they teach you in school? A monarch, like the queen, only more so. As you know, they have communism in Russia now, but before the revolution of 1917—"

"TELL THE STORY."

"All right. Two courtiers were telling the czar about a battle. But while they were talking, the czar fell asleep, so they started a conversation of their own. Prince Igor—who is really someone else from another story, but I'm borrowing him—said, 'I don't approve of corporal punishment'—just like your father, you know. And Prince Andrei—who is really from another story, too—said, 'Approve or not, how can you do without corporal punishment?' At that point, the czar woke up and said, 'Corporal punishment? What an unusual name! And how did this corporal make himself so indispensable?' Only that isn't really what they said, of course, because they were speaking Russian. What they said was '*Parootchiki zhe,*' which means, 'the lieutenants, however,' so the czar thought they were talking about someone called Lieutenant Showever."

"You're cheating!" Lolly objected. "It isn't a story about corporal punishment at all, really. I wanted a story about a kid getting hit for doing something wrong in school."

"All right, I'll get to that, in Corporal Punishment's school days. Meanwhile, see, the kind of story this is, it's music. Written by Prokofiev for a movie. So I want you to hear this music while you're in Russia, with the snow covering everything and still falling. It's bitter cold. In the distance, *very* far-off, there's a horn going 'DA da da, Da da da, Da da Daa Daa.' " I sang the opening melody. "Then there's a flute, going—"

"What does a flute sound like?" Lolly asked me, yawning.

"Oh, Lolly, you *know* a flute. High. Clear. Silvery. More like your voice than mine," and I sang her the flute part. She was asleep by the time the percussion came in.

* * *

The next morning, I found that Lolly's nightgown was definitely past mending. So when Max yelled down from his studio for a cup of coffee, I thought I'd try speaking to him again about getting her some clothes.

But I slipped on the little rug in front of the door, turning my ankle hard under me as I fell, breaking the mug, drenching myself in scalding coffee. I was shocked by all these things, and I was equally shocked by the word that flew out of my mouth. Generally, I found "hell" or "damn" perfectly adequate for the expression of my strongest feelings. Max had dropped his brush and bounded across the room to me. I was touched—momentarily—by what I thought was his solicitude. He slapped me across the face so hard that the side of my head, hitting the doorframe, was cut right open, and bled.

He had a rag in his hand, a rag with paint on it, and turpentine. He touched it to the cut on my temple; I screamed.

"I'm sorry," he said, "I didn't mean to hit you so hard. I just can't stand to hear a woman use that word. It's all right." He hugged me. "I love you. I didn't mean to hurt you."

If you didn't mean to hurt me, why did you hit me? I wondered. You didn't mean to hit me *so hard*, Mister Anti-Corporal-Punishment? And *you're* saying it's all right, *you're* forgiving *me*? I said only, "Let me go. I have to get a Band-Aid."

I took up six inches on the hem and sleeves of my spare flannel nightgown: Two Lollys would have fit in its width, but it would do. I put it on her pillow. By the time I had done that, there was no longer enough time to run to the bakery before she came home from school. Usually, I would give her one of the stale buns they sold there for a farthing for her tea.

"What happened to you?" she asked me, seeing the bandage.

"I fell down on that slippery rug in front of the door of the studio."

"Poor thing. Does it hurt?"

" 'Tis not so deep as a well, nor so wide as a church door, but 'tis enough, 'twill serve,' " I quoted, educational as ever.

"Well, where's my tea?"

"Lolly, I'm sorry, I forgot to go to the bakery."

"You silly—" and then Lolly said a word I didn't think she knew, a word I had first learned at the age of seventeen when I met it in a Ginsberg poem. It was enough to make one believe in astrology: first me, now little Lolly, foul-mouthed. I glanced up as though I expected Max to crash down on Lolly through the ceiling. I could see from Lolly's face that she had no idea what she'd said.

"Do you know what that word means, Lolly?"

"Oh, I didn't mean it, I'm sorry."

"But do you know what it means, what you just said?" I persisted.

"Well, a fool or something like that? I don't think you're a fool, really. I just want my tea."

"I know, Lolly. Now, listen, there are certain words that people say to hurt other people. What you just said is about the nastiest thing you can call a woman. And if someone called you that, it's as bad as if they'd hit you"; but when I said that, I wasn't sure whether it was true. "Did someone say that to you?"

She nodded. "What does it mean, exactly?"

"Well, it means a woman's—ah—private parts."

Lolly passed, the way children do, into hysterical giggling without any transition at all. Watching her, I wanted to laugh, too. Finally, she managed to gasp out, "You could have—an army—Private Parts—Corporal Punishment—General Rule."

"Major Medical!" I offered, joining in her giggles.

Max appeared at the head of the stairs. He had been hovering around me all day, not saying anything, appearing, disappearing, reappearing. "Or Major Offensive, which should it be, Lolly?"

"Let's have both!" she squealed.

"What's the joke, girls?" Max asked, with diffidence.

"Have tea with us, Daddy!" Lolly begged. Usually, Max stayed in his studio till dinnertime.

"We're making an army," Lolly explained, "with Corporal Punishment and General Rule and Private Pa—"

I was standing behind her chair. "Private Party," I said, kicking Lolly on the ankle.

She looked up at me quite startled, and I looked back seriously, warningly. After some silence, she said, "Major What-did-you-say? Major What?"

As I repeated the puns, I thought that someone's innocence was passing away as I spoke, but I didn't know whether it was Lolly's or mine.

"Think of one, Daddy," Lolly begged.

"If I do, can I have tea with you?" Max asked.

"Oh, you can have tea with us even if you don't!" Lolly told him. "*Please* have tea with us."

"I was asking your stepmother."

I looked down at Lolly.

"With me," said Max in a badly done accent, "I am bringing Colonel Oftruth. Is officer of very high ranking in KGB. Is not, perhaps, good company for ladies. Beeg bully."

I jerked my head ungraciously at the table. "But it's only toast and jam," I warned him as I went to the kitchen to put on the kettle.

GOSPEL FOR A PROUD SUNDAY

FOR TOM STEELE

I saw it. You've got to understand, it's embarrassing, because I can't exactly believe what I saw, but . . . I saw it.

It was Gay Pride Day. I was straggling down Fifth Avenue, feeling bad. I was tired and hung over, and as if that wasn't enough, I was heading for the office. Having to work on a Sunday is bad enough, but having to work on Gay Pride Day is the pits.

I didn't really want to march—I don't go in for that sort of thing—but I would have liked to be in on the fun when the parade was over. With all I had to do, though, I realized that by the time I could get to the Village, all that would be left was the drearier end of the aftermath. And that can be pretty dreary, believe me. In 1985, for example, I recall spending the fag-end, so to speak, of Gay Pride Day encircled by six shirtless and mindless trolls in front of Badlands. They were washing down ludes with beer, and had apparently been doing so all day. It wasn't just that they were all so flabbily unattractive, there was something really sinister about them. Something irrevocably damaged. I remember it struck me at the time that they were more nightmarish than anything that had ever appeared in my actual nightmares, but I was stuck in their company because my helpless cousin Horace from Philadelphia had suddenly said, "Wait here, Jeremy, I'll be right back," then disappeared for an hour and a half. And even though I didn't have Horace to worry about this time, the memory of that night was sort of putting me off going downtown at all.

But I couldn't really settle down into feeling sorry for myself about it, because I was standing in front of St. Patrick's and listening to the raving bigots. Watching all those earnest marchers going by that little clump of self-righteous hatred, I was starting to feel guilty for not joining them. Because every time I see a bunch of antigay demonstrators, I'm overwhelmed by the suspicion that that's what the whole country's made of, really—when you live in one of the pockets of resistance, like New York, it's too easy not to think about that. "It's not my fault I have to work," I tried telling myself, and by one of those coincidences more common in real life than in literature these days, a voice near me in the crowd, a voice with a slight foreign accent, said, "You could have done your work yesterday."

Naturally, I looked around to see who had said it. I've got to admit, he was the most beautiful man I've ever seen. His hair was nearly to his waist, and he was wearing a flowing white robe. That kind of hippie look ordinarily turns me off, but this guy was . . . exceptional. *Really* exceptional. And while I was just gaping at him, taking him in, he turned to the bigot in front of him, who was carrying a sign that said AIDS—GOD'S PUNISHMENT FOR GAYS, and knocked the sign out of his hand.

"How dare you?" he said. "How dare you say that about my father? And in the shadow of His house?"

A nut. I should have known from the way he was dressed. That's life. The most beautiful man I've ever seen turns out to be a lunatic.

I kept on going down Fifth Avenue, but I couldn't resist just glancing back for one more glimpse of the beautiful nut. He'd started a scuffle: He'd rolled up the sign he'd snatched and he was hitting some of the bigots with it and they were hitting him back with the poles from other signs and banners. Some of them kept up their ranting while they were fighting. Cops rushed over, but all of a sudden there seemed to be more fights breaking out on that corner than there were cops.

I was getting more and more depressed. I decided I needed something to eat before I started work, and though I hate tourist traps and they're so overpriced that just walking in one seems like some kind of treason to the human race, I found myself tottering into one of the worst of them because I thought I could convince myself I was still on my way to the office while sitting there at the counter, watching the parade out the window from a nice, air-conditioned ringside seat.

And I was just starting to feel a little better, halfway through a pastrami sandwich that could have been surpassed for half the price by the deli on my corner if only I'd had the forethought, when who should come stumbling in but the beautiful nut. Although the only other people at the counter were a couple of German tourists (the wife kept rushing out the door with her Leica whenever a notable costume appeared, but neither of them had smiled even once)—and although I had the end seat, farthest from the door—the nut slid onto the stool next to mine.

"You saw what happened," he said to me.

I'm nervous about getting into conversations with nuts, however beautiful, but since he'd seen me watching, I thought denying it would only provoke him, so I just nodded in a polite, noncommittal way and kept on eating my pastrami sandwich.

"I got away from the policemen," he said.

I nodded again, and kept right on chewing. It seemed like the safest thing to do.

"You are thinking I was overreacting?" he said, leaning in over me to bring his face closer to mine.

I shrugged diplomatically. I didn't really want anything to do with him, but there was something heady about the smell of his hair. I may have smiled.

He sighed. "Sometimes I lose my temper like that. When people are doing wicked things in the name of God, it gets to me, you know?"

I didn't want to get drawn into some insane theological discussion, but when the nut started talking about wicked things done in the name of God, I found my eyes sliding involuntarily over to the German tourists. The frau was squinting out the window at a sign (DOWN WITH KOCH AND THE GAY EMPIRE) carried by some straggling bigot on the sidewalk. "Down vit cock," she read earnestly. I didn't want to encourage the nut, but I had to smile.

He didn't seem to have noticed, though. "Once, long ago," he went on, "I did something like that. It was money changers right in the temple, can you imagine? But this, today, it's worse blasphemy; you should have helped to fight them, don't you think so?"

I realized that "Just who do you think you are?" was a question I had never in my life asked literally, but, since I knew the answer, there didn't seem to be any point in asking it. Besides, just then the waiter came over to give the nut a menu.

The nut raised his hand, palm toward the waiter, spurning the menu with a gesture I have often seen in devotional art. "Just give me a frankfurter," he said.

The waiter was young, but horribly emaciated, pathetically stooped, and sweating unwholesomely all over the menu he was holding. He stared deliriously at the nut, taking in the flowing hair and flowing robe. "Cost you eight ninety-five," he told him.

The nut sighed. "I know."

The waiter went away.

"I take the sins of the world on my shoulders," the nut was mumbling. I couldn't be sure whether he was talking about the price of the hot dog or the bigots he'd been fighting. "Gays are very dear to God," he went on.

I was getting pretty irritated, and besides, I was almost finished my sandwich and the nut had only just ordered, so I figured I didn't really have anything to lose by saying something to him. "That's not the way I heard it," was what I said. I thought of it as an exit line, more or less.

"What you heard was wrong. People amaze me sometimes. So obtuse, you know?"

A group from Dignity was going by the window, nuns and priests in front.

The nut pointed at them, smiling. "People understand how he loves sterility, don't they?"

"No," I said, really sorry I'd started talking to him. "They don't."

"That's what I mean. They're obtuse."

"People," I told him impatiently, "who believe in God seem to have the impression that there is something very antisexual about Him." Out the window, I could see masses of gay Christians marching, carrying banners identifying them by denomination. "Most of them, anyway." There's something really exasperating about finding yourself talking about God when you don't believe in any such thing.

"Well, they're very wrong, but I shouldn't really blame them. It's not easy to understand Him," the nut said. His voice wasn't like the usual nuts' voices you hear on the street: It was gentle, reasonable-sounding, and there was something really appealing in his unplaceable accent.

"I'm sure you can see why people aren't about to worship something they don't understand," I said. I was look-

ing for the waiter; I wanted to get my check and get out.
But there was no sign of him.

"They do that all the time," the nut told me.

"Maybe some of them do," I answered, "but not me,
okay? As far as I'm concerned, if God doesn't make sense,
He's not God, see?"

"You're kind of hung up on understanding, aren't you?
Haven't you ever noticed how limited it is? Can you tell
me why mercy is superior to efficiency?"

I shook my head, waiting for him to tell me the answer.

"I can't tell you, because it can't be explained. Not
everything can. But you know it's true."

I stood up, but he went on talking. "Would anything
that *wasn't* beyond your comprehension be worthy to be
called God? Would you really worship a being who had
your values? Think about it. Wouldn't you want something . . . superior?"

"Look," I told him, "I don't want to worship anything,
okay?"

The nut said, "Don't you want to get beyond your*self*?"

"Not particularly," I mumbled, thinking that I would
settle quite happily for getting beyond *him*, beautiful though
he was.

"You don't know what you want," the nut said.

"I do," I told him. "The check."

He ignored me. "When you feel guilty, like you were
feeling before, for not marching today, you are wanting to
get beyond yourself—isn't that true? Even when you think
the only thing you're wanting is sex, part of what you are
wanting is that same thing, to get beyond yourself—which
is why God likes sex, by the way."

"If God likes sex so much," I heard myself asking him,
"what about the destruction of Sodom?"

"Yes." The nut nodded. "He has rewarded gays from
the beginning."

"Rewarded?" I said, figuring this little exchange was
exactly what I deserved for speaking to him when I hadn't
meant to.

"Death," the nut explained, "is the best gift He has to give. Try to see it from His point of view: It's like a teacher letting kids out of school early."

"Oh, yeah?" I spluttered. "You told me why God lets the innocent die, you want to tell me why He lets them *suffer*?" I couldn't believe I was having this conversation. I don't think I've asked those questions since I was ten years old, and here I was, not just asking them—at my age—but asking them of some hippie lunatic off the street. It's not the kind of thing I do, believe me.

"Weren't you listening to me? I told you God didn't have your values. He wouldn't be God if He did. He'd be . . . you."

"Listen," I told him, "as far as I'm concerned, He wouldn't be God if He let certain things go on. And He has, and He does, so He isn't." I found my eyes sliding over to the German couple again, thinking of the Holocaust as I watched them scarfing down their deli food while marchers with pink triangles filed down Fifth Avenue in front of them. "So until I see Him stepping in to stop them, I'm not going to say there's a God."

"Even then, you won't," said the nut.

"What's that supposed to mean?" I wondered. I wasn't really asking him; I didn't really care.

Just then, the waiter finally appeared, with my check and the nut's meal. He looked awfully sick. Waxy. He was sweating worse than before, and trembling violently.

"It's supposed to mean that if you saw God intervene in human history, perform a miracle right before your eyes, you still wouldn't worship Him."

"Okay," I said meanly, getting the money out of my wallet to pay for my beer and my sandwich, "I'll make a deal with you. I understand who you're—ah—claiming to be. You perform a miracle, and I'll pay for your hot dog, pal, how's that?" (Herod was my favorite character in *Jesus Christ, Superstar*.) "I'd appreciate it if you'd be quick about it; I have to get in to the office, and I've already wasted quite a bit of time here."

The nut nodded. He looked at the waiter, who was putting mustard in front of him with shaking hands. "I can cure you," he said. "Do you believe me?"

The waiter moaned. "I'll believe anything. Hey, you got AL721? Listen, I can pay."

"You are cured," the nut told him. "You are well. Could you bring me a little sauerkraut?"

And the thing is, this waiter—I mean, it wasn't just that he straightened up and stopped shaking and sweating, but he swelled up. I saw it, I saw this skeletal, pathetic kid round out like someone was inflating him. He must have put on fifty pounds in five seconds—it was like watching a plant grow in a time-lapse movie. Or the Incredible Hulk on television. Muscles popped out on his arms, on his chest. All of a sudden, he was a gorgeous kid, the kind it breaks your heart to pass on a beach. He looked extremely, glowingly, radiantly healthy, and a little dazed. I don't think he knew what had happened. Because all he said was, "Sure. You want something to drink?"

"You going to pay for that, too?" the nut turned to me to ask.

I was speechless. I just nodded. It was all I was capable of. I don't even think my mouth was closed. I couldn't even tell you exactly what happened next; I was just kind of taking it in, realizing what I'd just seen. I think the waiter brought the nut his sauerkraut, and a beer. I think I paid for it. I know that eventually I found I was able to speak, because I remember very clearly saying, "It happened. It really happened, then, all that in the Bible."

And I remember the nut said, "Of course it happened."

"All those miracles. Healing the sick, making the lame walk and the blind see, raising the dead," I said.

The nut nodded, with one of those little self-deprecating shrugs people give when you mention their achievements.

"It's goddamned obscene," I told him. "You *could* save them, but you'd rather let the innocent suffer, whole nations at a time—did I say *let* them? You get off on it! You know how many people have AIDS right here in this city right now? You could actually cure them all, couldn't you? But no, you won't, will you? Only if you happened to feel like showing off, you might take some poor sod like Lazarus and raise him from the dead. Or single out one waiter to cure so you can cadge a hot dog from a stranger. I mean, it's so fucking *arbitrary.*"

"You think *I'm* arbitrary," said the nut. "You should see my father."

So I hit him. I knocked him right off the stool and walked out the door without looking back. On my way out, I heard him saying, "Forgive them, for they know not what they do."

I couldn't just go on into the office and settle down to work as if nothing had happened. And the parade was still going by. So I wound up marching after all.

NUDES BEYOND GENDER

FOR ATHOS DEMETRIOU

Trashing paintings is one of my favorite things. Besides, I find it reassuring when other people share my aversions. So when I spotted Fleur at the Whitney, standing in front of an Alex Katz and obviously disgusted with it, I couldn't resist joining her. She was talking to an ugly little man who hates Katz as much as I do. After he left us, I asked her, since she had never introduced him, "Who was that guy? He seemed kind of familiar, but—"

"That was Nick the—"

"Nick the what?" I naturally wanted to know.

"Nick Theopopolis," Fleur said. But Fleur is so guileless (and it is only her simplicity that enables me to forgive her for making such bad art) that she couldn't hide the fact that she had been about to tell me something about this Nick, and then thought better of it.

So I jumped to the conclusion that he must be a Potentially Useful Person whom Fleur wanted to keep to herself. Looking back on it, that was silly of me, because of course Fleur is not only too decent and well-meaning to even think of making use of anybody, but also not bright enough to do it if she wanted to. But, at the time, that did not occur to me, and I thought Fleur must be holding back something along the lines of "Nick the *Art News* critic," or "Nick the scout for Mary Boone."

I thought that if Nick was Anybody, it would be easy enough to find out Who, either from someone other than Fleur (now that I knew Nick's name) or from Nick himself (now that I had a precedent for talking to him). Given her helplessness, it would have been easy enough to get Fleur to tell me what she'd been about to say, but conversations with Fleur always wind up uncomfortable. She always presses me for judgments of her paintings, and it's difficult to find something to tell her that is neither untruthful nor cruel. So I escaped before she could ask me whether I'd seen the latest of her sickly sweet abominations, which were on view with works by other members of her female artists' collective.

Now that I had a name to attach to Nick's face, I found myself recognizing him here and there around town from time to time. But we always seemed to be on opposite sides of crowded rooms. It was nearly six weeks before I had a chance to talk to him again, and by that time, I'd found out he was only a fellow artist. God knows, there's not much use in *them*, so apart from wondering fleetingly why, in that case, Fleur hadn't told me whatever it was she hadn't told me, I forgot all about him.

But then I found him at my elbow one day in the Met. I'd tagged along with my friend Julian, who was writing something about Lorenzo di Credi and had to stare at that *Portrait of a Lady* till he could invent some explanation of the mysterious gesture she's making with the ring. I got bored watching him look at the di Credi, so I said I'd meet him in front of the newly acquired Lotto (which neither of us had seen) in an hour, and wandered aimlessly through the museum till I found myself next to Nick with a Georgia O'Keeffe in front of us.

"I *hate* her," I said, by way of greeting, because I do.

Nick nodded. His expression became very serious. He is far from prepossessing, and that expression was particularly unbecoming. He is young, but because he is fat, and heavily pockmarked, his face and body present a series of sagging configurations. Besides that, his hair is thick, straight, long, and so gooily plastered down that it suggests a pair of drooping ears. When his face goes solemn, his resemblance to a basset hound is almost painful.

"Why?" he asked, radiating baleful respect.

"Pornography for the *Reader's Digest* crowd," I snorted, making a contemptuous, dismissive gesture at the canvas in front of us. "Hyperbolic euphemism."

He nodded. This motion caused his neck to disappear completely.

I found myself feeling a bit sheepish. Every time this man talks to me, I thought, I am denouncing some artist. I *do* hate Katz, I do hate O'Keeffe, but am I really trying to share my vision and uphold my standards, or am I just strutting my stuff? I needed to say something nice about someone, to prove I wasn't just another bitter old show-off.

"Oh, Nick," I was relieved to be able to tell him, "I saw your *Digital Watch* series at Vitelli's. It was really quite good—I loved those green knuckles. Are you showing anything now?"

"Yeah, well, I've got a few things at Schram. I'm one of the owners, so it's kind of . . . but . . . they're there."

So, this little man owns a gallery, does he? I thought, and I found myself taking a new interest in Nick, and wondering whether that's what Fleur had thought better of telling me. "Same kind of thing you had at Vitelli's? More fingers?" I put these questions eagerly enough to suggest that my view of the universe could be transformed by his artistic development.

"More or less." Nick shrugged, causing his neck to

vanish again. "I guess you could call me a neoexpressionist."

"You neoexpressionist, you," I said.

He laughed. He has a beautiful laugh, actually, bass-baritone, as rich and sweet as a butterscotch sundae. But what I said wasn't that funny—could it be, I wondered, that *he* thinks *I* might be useful?

"Forgive me," he said then, as if to confirm my suspicion, "I've talked to you before—I remembered what you said about Alex Katz—very, ah, perceptive, but I don't know your name."

"That's okay," I said, thinking I was about to dispel his interest forever, "no one does. It's Shelby, Shelby Hillyard."

He seized my hand and pressed it with unaccountable enthusiasm.

"You're an artist?"

I nodded, modestly. How else could I nod, in answer to that particular question? "Not a very successful one, I'm afraid."

"How can that be?" he crooned. "You know, the first thing I ever noticed about you—oh, I've seen you around, and I've always noticed your hands. Wonderful, expressive hands. They look capable of great things."

I was absolutely nonplussed. Why the hell was this man coming on to me? I must be ten years older than he is, God knows I'm no beauty, and he'd just learned how unimportant I am.

"I think they're hideous," I said, bewildered. "So long and spindly and masculine."

"You take good care of them, though."

"Oh, I just can't stand paint under my nails. Makes me think I'm probably not a Real Artist—you know?"

"You have to stop being so hard on yourself," Nick urged me. "And you look at art very intelligently; I think you must be better than you think. Listen, would you let me take a look at some of your work?"

Would I *let* him? Dear God, the man owns a gallery.

I would *pay* him to look at my work. I would— I began to rummage in my purse. I found the card, and gave it to him. "I have a painting at this gallery," I muttered, "but I don't suppose you ever find yourself on the Upper West Side."

"Oh, I'll make a point of it," he assured me, giving me a look of what I can only call ardent interest. But, I thought, it *couldn't* be, it must be the way the light is bouncing off his contacts or something, an illusion.

I felt the need to get away before we could have any further conversation about my painting and where it is. It's sort of embarrassing: I'm not ashamed of the painting, it's pretty good, but it isn't in a proper gallery at all. These two guys I know are running a business out of their apartment; they deal in what they call homoerotic art, which my painting could, accidentally, be read as being. It's there because one day someone looked at it and said, "You know, I'll bet Ron and Jamie would take that thing," and they did. To my amazement, because by that time I had resigned myself to painting strictly as a hobby. I was really exhilarated, thinking of total strangers walking around Ron and Jamie's apartment, looking at my *Ephebe,* just like Posterity looking at a Rembrandt.

I didn't want to start describing Ron and Jamie's business to Nick, though, so I was glad to be able to say, "I'm afraid someone's waiting for me in European Painting." I didn't think Nick would really go look at my picture; I figured he was just being polite.

But then Nick said, "Shelby, are you going to Howard MacKenzie's opening on Saturday?"

(Who the hell is Howard MacKenzie?) "Ah—"

"Because I was wondering if you'd let me take you to lunch first, maybe we could go there together?"

Is there a creature on this earth who I wouldn't allow to buy me a meal? We agreed to meet at Berry's, and I straggled away in a daze, feeling an urgent need to look in a mirror but somehow not liking to pull one out in public.

I found Julian in front of the Lotto. He turned to me

with a radiant smile, inviting me to share his appreciation. But I was too perturbed even to look at the painting. "Julian," I blurted, "do you think I'm attractive? For my age, I mean?"

"Jesus Christ!" he hissed. "Women! I walk through this museum and wonder how I have the gall to write about these miracles, and you—"

"No, Julian, there's a reason," I tried to explain, feeling somehow robbed of the ability to put words together coherently. "There's this man, he's an artist, actually, Nick Theopopolis?"

Julian's face was all blank impatience.

"Well, he's one of the owners of this gallery, Schram; have you ever heard of it?"

"Was that where they had those really regrettable Gilbert and Georges last year?"

"I don't know," I said, thinking, Oh, my God, could I conceivably have a chance of showing in a gallery where they've shown Gilbert and George? "I wish I understood what you have against them."

"Shelby, my dear, Life is Life and Art is Art."

"How can you be so sure? But Julian, this man Nick?—he's behaving like he's—I don't know—*smitten* with me or something. He asked me to lunch."

Julian shrugged. "Good for you," he said quizzically.

"He's short and fat and ugly. Even so, why would anybody that young—he must be *your* age—be paying that kind of attention to me? I mean, he doesn't even know me."

"You've always had your admirers, darling," Julian pointed out.

"Yes, but they're people like you, who've known me for ages. I mean, if I have any admirable qualities, I don't think they're that *conspicuous*. It doesn't make sense, Julian. He said I had wonderful *hands*." I waggled one of them in Julian's face.

He raised one of his to meet it, slapping his palm on mine. "They *are* conspicuous," he said. "Look, my hands are in proportion to my body. Your hand, Shelby, is exactly the same size as mine." I had to admit it was. As he lowered his hand, I looked sadly up to the top of his head, a full foot above me. "Freak," he chuckled.

"He said I looked at art intelligently?" I told Julian in a questioning way.

"So you do, so you do, it's the only reason I put up with you," he said. "Now how about looking intelligently at this Venus with me? Isn't it lovely?"

It was, of course, but I felt abruptly embarrassed by the shameless celebration of flesh. I was in the mood for something more fearful—say, Francis Bacon.

"I do like his work, actually, what I've seen of it," I mumbled.

"Lotto isn't rated as highly as he—"

"No, no, I meant Nick's," I explained. "Oh, dear. I'd like him for a friend, actually, but I don't think I can return whatever feeling he seems to . . ."

"So what is the problem?" Julian wondered.

"I'll never get anywhere," I said gloomily. "I always think I'm desperate and ruthless, but whenever I get a chance to be, I'm not."

By Saturday, I was in a state of witless nervousness. I started our lunch together by spilling a glass of water on the tablecloth and Nick's pants.

"Oh, I'm sorry," I stammered. "I'm so clumsy." I had come to the halfhearted conclusion that Nick's interest couldn't really be as ardent as I had thought. The way someone looks at you is always ambiguous, after all. Brooding on the words he had actually spoken, I thought I must have turned into one of those lonely middle-aged women who begin to imagine all sorts of things about polite, unmeant gallantry.

But then Nick said, "How could those beautiful hands be clumsy? You never wear rings on them, do you?"

"Sure, sometimes, I've been known to."

"But you seem like a free spirit," Nick said.

"What does that have to do with wearing rings?" I asked.

"You're not married, are you?"

I shook my head, and then somehow I got up the gumption to ask, "If I were married, what would I be doing letting a strange man—well, I don't mean you're strange, but . . ." I felt that I was putting my question very badly.

His eyes sunk to the tablecloth. His neck, as so often, was gone. "I had a bad experience once with a woman. . . . Do you have a boyfriend?"

I waved my hands in front of his face, as though to stop a car that was speeding down a road. I guess I gesture a lot; I felt throttled by Nick's making me too aware of my hands. "Look," I said, altogether robbed of poise, "there are a lot of men I see socially, but they're—well, they're friends, they're all people I know very well—maybe I'm in something of a rut, come to think of it, but I don't have a boyfriend, as such. I mean, I don't *date* anybody, the very idea seems, well, it isn't very grown-up. I'd feel silly, at my age."

"All right," Nick said, "how old are you? Out with it."

"Forty," I said.

"That makes no difference to me." He smiled.

"How old are you?" I asked, thinking, I am not imagining things, this is not reflexive chivalry.

"Thirty-one. Were you ever married, Shelby?"

So much, I thought, for the hope of showing my paintings at Schram.

"Nick," I said, "look, I don't *date*, like I told you; I don't know the rules for this kind of conversation—if there are any—but frankly, you are making me *very* nervous. I mean, I've only spoken to you a couple of times, and I just can't feel comfortable with all these personal compliments and personal questions when I hardly know you."

"Oh, I don't know the rules, either. You just put me in my place if I do anything wrong, okay?"

"Well, I don't think you've done anything I could call

wrong, exactly, it's just that you make me very self-conscious, and I don't understand you."

We stared at each other for a while.

"I saw your painting," he said, finally.

"You did?" I felt that an opportunity was being offered to me, and that I was inadequate to it.

"Brava!" he smiled. "It's terrific. *Nice* observation, intelligently composed—beautiful texture, too."

"Oh," I said, "thank you." I waited to hear myself ask him whether he would consider showing anything of mine, but I didn't hear myself ask it.

I have two consciences. They're physical, organic. One of them is in the front part of my right temple, and it decides on simple matters of right and wrong. The other one is right in between my lungs, and it agonizes over choosing between the lesser of any given set of evils. It was the one over my temple that wouldn't let me say a word about showing my work at Schram.

Nick and I spent the rest of the meal talking about other people's art, almost entirely about art we didn't like. We seemed to share a lot of opinions.

Then we went to the MacKenzie opening, and Nick dumped me at the door and abandoned me. I found a lot of people I knew to talk to, but I found his behavior puzzling. After a couple of hours, I decided to go. It seemed only polite to inform him—after all, he brought me. So I went up to him, and found he was talking to Fleur, whom I hadn't seen in quite a while.

"Let me walk you to a cab," Nick said, kissing Fleur's hand—presumably by way of farewell.

"Oh, no," I said, "don't let me drag you away, you're having a good time. I'm taking the subway, anyhow. So, ah, thanks for lunch, and thanks for bringing me."

"Are you busy next Saturday night?"

I could have told him I would be busy. After all, I am always busy, I don't know how not to be. I have a busy temperament. But I said, "No, I don't think so, no."

"Would you let me take you to dinner?"

(Again, would I *let* him!) "Yes, thank you, yes."

I noticed Fleur was looking at me in an odd way, sort of speculative. It is not like Fleur to speculate.

So the next day I called her and said, "Tell me about Nick. Did you ever go out with him?"

"Oh, no," she said, "I never really went out with him—I mean, one date. We're just friends. Are you seeing Nick?"

"One lunch. That's hardly *seeing* someone—what a curious expression that is, isn't it? But I said I'd go out with him on Saturday, and he seems kind of strange. I don't know what to make of him. So tell me what you know."

"He's . . . he's actually a very charming guy. And a talented painter."

"Not about his painting, Fleur. Personal."

"Well, I don't know if I should tell you this—"

"Spill it."

"Oh, I don't know him all that well, really. It's just that I have this friend? And I went out with him once, and she went out with him once, and . . ."

I waited a decent interval. "And?" I finally asked.

"I think he's maybe, like there's something wrong with him, you know?"

"What exactly?" I not unnaturally wanted to know.

For a while I could hear Fleur breathing into the receiver. Then I heard her say, "I think he's afraid of emotional commitment."

"I don't see anything wrong with that," I told her. "It is rather terrifying. Fleur, when you went out with him, did he—I don't know how to put this, but did he start out with the kind of thing you expect from someone who's had more time to get to know you?"

But as soon as I said it, I wondered what was the point of asking Fleur that. Fleur is a fluffy, pretty little thing, very young and sweet and not frightfully bright. She's all on the surface, so what else could anyone respond to in her?

She told me, "He was talking like he really liked my painting and he really wanted to see me again, but he never called me after that night. And he was kind of—aggressive. I mean, it was the only time I'd ever been out with him, and he kept saying what exquisite, delicate little hands I had, and trying to grab them under the table."

"Oh, yeah?" I said. "He keeps telling me what wonderful hands I have, and he did kind of lunge at one, too."

"And the thing is, when he went out with my friend, he did the same thing. He tried to kiss me, too," Fleur went on. "On the first date—I thought that was kind of . . ."

I waited for her to find a word until I realized she wasn't going to.

"And the same with your friend?" I asked.

"Yeah," she said. "Creepy, isn't it? But," she went on without giving me a chance to reply, "he might be different with someone like you. You might be good for him."

"How do you mean? In the first place, I'm old enough to be his mother . . ."

"How old *are* you?" Fleur asked. She doesn't understand hyperbole.

"Forty, forty, forty." Everyone seemed to be asking that question. I was starting to feel like Blanche du Bois. "Why do you think I'd be good for him?"

"Oh, you're so sure of yourself. You wouldn't let him get away with anything."

It was comforting to think I seemed sure of myself to someone, even to someone as fluff-headed as Fleur. And I found it flattering, in a perverse kind of way, that any man, even a man like Nick, could even think of wanting to treat me like a silly, pretty young girl.

"Fleur, how old was the friend of yours that went out with Nick?"

"Oh, she's much younger than I am. Twenty-three."

(Fleur has just turned twenty-five.) "I think it would be different for you. Maybe you could give him a taste of his own medicine."

"How do you mean?" I wondered.

"Aren't you in love with Julian Booth?"

Fleur is so damnably simple.

That week, I found myself wondering what would happen on Saturday night. On Wednesday, though, Jamie called me to tell me someone had bought my painting, and I forgot all about Nick. I was ecstatic. After Ron and Jamie had taken their cut, I had almost five hundred dollars: the first money I'd ever earned for my very own, noncommercial (dig this capital A!) Art. And Jamie wanted more! More! Did I have any more male nudes?

"Yeah, I'll have to dig them up," I told him, knowing I didn't have anything of the kind, but figuring I could take Thursday and Friday off from work, paint all weekend, and have three—maybe even four—more paintings ready by Monday.

On Thursday afternoon, while I was painting, my doorbell rang. It was Julian.

"Where the hell have you been?" he actually yelled.

He's not a yeller. I was amazed.

"Right here," I told him.

"I've been *calling* you," he said.

"I unplugged it," I explained. I waved a brush at him. "I'm painting."

"You *forgot,*" he said, glowering.

"Forgot what?"

"The preview at the Morgan? You promised to go with me, remember?"

"Oh, Julian, I'm sorry, I'm so sorry, I did forget, yes, I completely forgot. Oh, Julian, dearie, look, I'll make it up to you somehow. You'd better go on by yourself. I have to paint—"

"What *are* you doing?" Julian asked, looking horrified at the canvas in front of me.

"Sex-change operation," I told him.

"It's your *Graces*—I don't believe you're doing that. Look, you've completely ruined the composition. Damn it, Shelby, what's the matter with you?"

"I'm not finished yet," I said. "It's coming along, though. I think they'll be quite handsome when I'm done," but even while saying it, I realized that he had a point about the composition. Now that they were gone, I could see that the breasts had been quite important to the balance of the thing.

" 'Handsome!' My dear, how long has it been since you looked at a male body? That fellow in front is shaped like a pear."

"Michelangelo used male models for his women," I protested, but without conviction.

"That doesn't mean you can do what you're doing," Julian said wearily. "And may I point out that in the market you're prostituting your talent for, hips like that are not in great demand?"

I put down the brush. "Pose for me, Julian? Ten minutes?"

"Certainly not!" he squawked. "Clean yourself up to go to the preview. We're already an hour late. I need a female, damn it. Fred Jarvis is going to be there. The man could make my career. He wants to talk to me about Crivelli, but he's notoriously homophobic; I have to show up with a *girl*."

"Oh, you're paranoid about that, Julian; I'm sure he doesn't care. And I'm not even a plausible girl, I'm forty years old. Maybe Jeanie downstairs would go with you; let's call her." Fleetingly, I remembered what Fleur had told me about Nick, and I found myself wondering why I should bother resenting such a thing—no doubt one woman *is* as good as another, for most purposes.

"You're perfectly plausible—even impressive, once you open your mouth." Julian said it grudgingly, but I was really pleased. The depressing thought of Nick was completely expunged. "Besides," he went on, "why would anyone want to take Jeanie to an event like that?"

"Because she's so drop-dead gorgeous," I told him sweetly. "Anyone would want to take her anywhere." But I was cleaning the paint off my hands as I spoke.

And when Julian and I got to the Morgan, the first person we saw, out on the corner before we even went inside, was Nick. I said, "Hi," he said, "Hi," and then proceeded to ignore me for the rest of the evening. Well, why not? It's not as if we had any kind of understanding; both of us had gone there with other people, and I was pretty busy helping Julian impress Fred Jarvis. Still, I was vaguely hurt that Nick never glanced my way. It reminded me, vividly, of the way he'd taken me to the MacKenzie opening and then abandoned me.

I complained about Nick to Julian. He was preoccupied. "Maybe he didn't see you; go over and talk to him." I heard him add, under his breath, *"women,"* as I went hesitantly off in Nick's direction.

Once I'd reached him, I took a deep breath, and said, "Well, what does a girl have to do to get your attention?"

"Wear a beautiful dress like that," he said.

This, of course, was a lie, and I should have pointed that out to him, but both of my consciences, the one in the temple and the one between the lungs, started acting up. I was confused.

"I'm exhausted," Nick went on, "just about ready to head home."

"Oh," I said, "well, I have a dinner party to go on to." (Fred Jarvis had actually asked me and Julian to go on to a restaurant with him and a few other people.)

"Oh," Nick said, and yet another disfiguring expression—one I couldn't identify—came over his features. Some variety of resentment? "Well, I'll see you Saturday. Will you be home if I give you a call in the afternoon?"

I'm not sure why, but I felt absolutely certain that he wouldn't have said that, that he would have forgotten our date entirely, if I hadn't said I was going on to a dinner party. At that rate, I really wanted him to see me leave with Julian, who is a beautiful man by anyone's standards, and Fred Jarvis, who is so much more important than Nick could ever hope to be, but Nick left at once, so I didn't get the chance to impress him with my exit. Watching Nick's, I pointed out to Julian that some men *are* shaped like pears.

"But no one wants to look at pictures of them," Julian said. "Shelby, do you *like* that man? He's repulsive."

"I'm not sure if I like him. He *is* repulsive, I grant you—still, he has a lovely voice, and looks aren't really very important, are they?"

Julian looked at me with a kind of wonder.

"I don't know, Julian, I think he gratifies some very perverse kind of vanity. And I hear he's unscrupulous. I respect that."

Julian just shook his head. I had the feeling he wanted to say more, but he didn't want to upset me and risk impairing my ability to make polite conversation with the Jarvises.

On Saturday at dinner, Nick ran into a couple he knew at the restaurant. They joined us for a while, and I found I was getting a better impression of Nick. When he wasn't doing his male-animal bit, he seemed to be a very likable sort of human being—intelligent, funny, and kind.

After dinner, he said he'd walk me to a cab, and I said, "No, I'm taking the subway." He started walking more slowly, and tried to kiss me as we were passing through a dark patch of street.

It must be a very becoming patch of street. Nick is actually the fourth man who's tried to kiss me on that block, but the last time that happened was three years ago. "Don't kiss me, Nick," I said.

We walked on in embarrassed silence. "Would you like a cup of coffee?" he asked. I thought, If his neck is showing, I will, but it was too dark in the street to tell.

"All right," I said.

Once we were seated in a coffee shop, I said, "Look,

Nick, I don't understand you. You frighten me, I don't understand this kind of sudden attraction," and while I said it I wondered what was the matter with me—why couldn't I deal with him more honestly?

"Those beautiful hands." He sighed, and seized one.

"I'll bet you say that to all the girls," I muttered, but I didn't pull it away.

"I'm a simple kind of guy," he said. All at once it seemed awfully sordid that I was letting him hold my hand. In my experience, whenever a man has told me how simple he is, he's meant one of two things. And I knew Nick couldn't be hungry, because he had just finished a big dinner.

"Well, I'm not," I said, "I'm complicated. Maybe you were misled by that picture of mine. It was nice of you to go and see it, by the way; I didn't think you would."

"You told me not to kiss you," he pointed out, "but you didn't move away."

"Oh, dear," I said, "am I being skittish or something?"

"The time will come when I'll get skittish. I wonder what you'll do about it," Nick said.

"So we'll be remembering this conversation at some time in the future?" I asked, amazed, thinking, I can't have talked to this man for more than three hours altogether. It's like walking in on a movie in the middle—here is a very improbable couple in mid-romance, how did they get there? All at once, Nick's ugliness seemed so pitiable that I felt guilty for noticing it. "I must tell you," I said gently. "I'm not in the market for a boyfriend."

He looked shocked. I thought that was odd.

"I really cherish being alone," I explained.

"Do you think I won't let you alone?" he asked. Present tense, I thought, he actually regards this as an ongoing relationship.

Had some sort of courtship been taking place while my attention was wandering? Had it been conducted on some level too subtle for me to understand? Or was he confusing me with some other woman? And if one of these hypotheses was correct, had the same one been true in Fleur's case, too? And her young friend's?

I didn't know what to say. This seldom happens to me: The novelty of the sensation was not disagreeable. I stood up. "It's late, Nick," I told him. "I have a lot of painting to do tomorrow, I really have to get home."

"I'll call you next weekend," he crooned, but of course he never did.

I botched the nudes so badly that I had to call Jamie and tell him they'd been destroyed in a flood in the basement of my building. Then I forgot all about them until Fleur found them in my closet one day when she'd come over to borrow some gesso.

"Hey, wow!" she kept clucking. "Hey, wow! These are *wonderful,* these kind of hermaphrodite things. Listen, let me take these in to the women artists' collective? I thought you said you hated feminist art! But these have got to be, like, allegories. Do they have titles?"

"*Nudes Beyond Gender,*" I said rather nastily.

"Hey, wow!" she said. "It's the feminine experience in our time, right?"

I was about to tell her the truth, but then I thought better of it. I had learned something from Nick after all.

"This, Fleur," I told her severely, "is postfeminist art. It is no longer meaningful to talk of the feminine experience. In our time, gender has been abolished. We reached a point where we were no longer men or women, only individuals. But we have passed that point. Having transcended gender, we must go on to transcend individuality. It is time for us to become completely interchangeable."

"Hey, wow!" said Fleur. Then she frowned.

M I L D E W

F O R   J U L I E   G R A Y

We were having a long rainy season. We hadn't seen the sun for seventeen days. What I minded most was the mildew. One day, my husband's little sister Fuyuko pulled her shoes out of the shoe case as she was leaving for school, gave a little shriek, and dropped them. They were completely covered with mold, inside and out.

Mildew on leather has a special character. It is something like what you find on a long-forgotten leftover at the back of the refrigerator: thick, fuzzy, greenish. Although it smells like wet animals, it's powdery, easy to brush off. You can even blow some of it away, like dandelion fluff.

I opened the shoe case, and all our shoes were covered with the stuff. The door stuck halfway open; the wood had swollen with the moisture in the air. I didn't understand it, because I put so much charcoal in the cupboard —it's supposed to retard mildew—and, for good measure, every time a packet of silica gel came into the house, I'd clean off the crumbs of whatever it came with (cookies, *o-sembei*, squid chips, or whatever) and tape it inside the shoe case.

After Fuyuko left, I cleaned all the shoes thoroughly. And polished them. That took all morning. Rubbing away, inhaling the sour air, I kept wondering how four people could possibly have acquired so many shoes. The next morning, all of them were covered with a fresh layer of mildew.

And in the afternoon I tried to clean the living room. I started by shoving the sofa forward, and found a huge blotch of mildew on the wall behind it, shaped just like the back of the sofa. This mildew wasn't fluffy. It seemed altogether different from what grew on the shoes. It was damp and brownish. It coated the wall thinly, but it clung. It hardly smelled at all, but there was something sinister in the faintness of its acrid odor. I had to scrub it off, and I dried the wall afterward, but by the time I had worked my way around the room and everything was swept or dusted or polished there was a new blotch of mildew where the old one had been.

I complained to my mother-in-law. I was starting to suspect that there was some simple way of getting rid of mildew, something that everyone else in Japan knew about and used. If that was the case, though, my mother-in-law would never have told me about it. For three years, she had let me struggle with wrinkling, buckling shoji paper. Finally, a neighbor told me to spray the paper with hot water. I did, and as it dried it shrank smooth and taut. I asked my mother-in-law why she had never told me to do that. "You have your own ways of doing things," she'd said.

She'd never forgiven Saburo for marrying an American. She thought he was letting the family down, and she said so, often. When I accused her of enjoying my failures, she'd pretend not to understand my Japanese.

She said the mildew was particularly bad because of the unremitting monsoons. "Seventeen days with no sun at all . . . it's unusual. I remember once, before the war, a *tsuyu* that lasted for a whole month, but there were a few clear days. At the first glimpse of the sun, everyone ran out into their gardens with laundry, bedding, they even took up the floors. The gardens were buried! But in that way, it was possible to keep the mildew under control." I found it hard to believe that one short interval of sun could make much of a dent in a dampness that had been accumulating for so long, permeating everything so thoroughly, but I hoped for one all the same.

The persistent rain cooped us all up together. We got on each other's nerves. Fuyuko couldn't hang out with her classmates in the afternoons, my mother-in-law couldn't toddle off to Bunraku shows or storytellers with her contemporaries, Saburo came straight home from work. We'd all sit around the living room together. The air was heavy with soured moisture. I never hung laundry in the living room, but hanging in all the other rooms, never really drying, it held that smell, which underlay the soon-staled smoke from Saburo's cigarettes.

I complained, that night, about the Hydra-like nature of the mildew.

"But it is good to keep busy," my mother-in-law said.

Before we could start squabbling, Saburo suggested that I help Fuyuko with her English homework.

I made a face at him. I appreciated his staving off the bickering, but there he was, getting credit with his mother and his sister for altruism and responsibility, when in fact he wanted to hear me speaking English because he found it sexy. Boredom always made him lecherous: I knew what he was up to.

"What are you reading?" I asked Fuyuko gamely enough.

"Lafcadio Hearn. Why do they teach us English with Japanese stories? What kind of English is that?" Fuyuko said. She was sprawling on the floor. She rolled over on her tummy to get the text out of her bookbag. But after finding it, she slid it under the table. "Don't you have some real English for me to read? Can I read something from *The Japan Times*? Or do you have an American letter?"

I had an American letter, one that had come that day, but I didn't want to read it with Fuyuko. For one thing, my correspondent asked how was the Yellow Peril, which is what I had taken to calling my mother-in-law in letters home. Besides, it was full of gossip about the adulteries and abortions of former college classmates. I wanted to forget that letter anyway. The last page was a headache-generating rationalization; my old friend had deserted her adolescent radicalism for what she called "big bucks."

"You got a letter today," my mother-in-law said.

"All this rain," I said. "I couldn't read it. It was soaked right through. The ink . . ." I trailed off. My Japanese suddenly failed me. "Ran," I would have said in English. But in Japanese, especially if you are a woman, it is polite to leave sentences unfinished. This is a disincentive to fluency. Besides, any sentence that ends unexpectedly is like the noise of the tree falling in the forest where no one can hear it.

"What a pity!" Fuyuko said. It seemed to me that her intonation was sarcastic, that she suspected I was concealing something juicy. "What about *The Japan Times*, then?"

"Maybe later," I temporized. "It's more important to do your homework, don't you think?"

But the fact was, I scarcely looked at *The Japan Times* anymore. I still didn't know enough characters to read a Japanese newspaper, but Tokyo's English-language daily was coming to seem even more foreign. The last time I had tried to read it, I had crumpled it up in disgust. It was full of words I didn't know: "aerobics," "streakers," "conceptualist." Even words I knew were used in incomprehensible combinations: "gay rights," "word processor," "coke spoons."

"So," Fuyuko said in English. "We are reading 'The Mujin.' "

I put my hand out for the book.

"Remember?" Fuyuko asked. "When you first came here? When Hide-chan thought you were a *mujin*?"

We all laughed at the memory, even my mother-in-law, who needed no translation to know what we were talking about after hearing "Hide-chan" and *"mujin."*

It was cozy, the family chuckling together, yet the recollection chilled me. This is what we were remembering: Not long after I arrived in Japan, I met the child of a neighbor who lived near the station. He was only a toddler then, and had naughtily ventured beyond his garden gate. I saw him come out, I knew his mother, so I thought I should greet him. I bowed and said hello to him in Japanese, and he ran howling back into the house, screaming "Mama! Mama! I saw a ghost, I saw a monster, I saw a *mujin!* Out there in the road! An enormous creature, dressed like a woman, with no eyes at all!"

Blue eyes are no eyes in Japan. Fuyuko, in the backyard of a classmate's house next door, had heard it all, and translated it gleefully when she came home. Since then, she called me *"Mujin-chan"* ("Dear Mujin") whenever I was behaving in some particularly foreign way.

The story of the *mujin* is very unsatisfactory to Western sensibilities, like so many Japanese folktales. It has no plot.

A traveler crosses a bridge and finds himself in an unfamiliar village. A swirling mist prevents him from seeing, but hearing the noise of wooden sandals, he realizes he is not alone on the street. He calls out to the passerby and asks directions to an inn. The mist lifts, and our hero discovers that the passerby has no face: He realizes that he has been talking to a *mujin.* And that, infuriatingly enough, is all. A *mujin* has a head, you understand, but where there should be features, there is only smooth flesh.

Fuyuko was reading this story, in the loud monotone she used for reading English, when the phone rang. My head was aching violently from the moist, motionless air, the drumming of the rain on the roof, Saburo's accumulated smoke, the stink of the mildew, the nagging suspicion that my country had changed unrecognizably since I left it. I tried to listen to Fuyuko's reading and to what my mother-in-law was saying on the telephone, yet I couldn't stop thinking of the letter I'd lied about. Rain-streaked though it had been, it had been easy to decipher, if not to understand.

The writer had been my roommate the year I met Saburo. "You know," she'd been the first to notice, and say, "that little Jap's in love with you."

I hadn't believed her. "You think so?" I'd said. "Then I should marry him. What an opportunity!"

"For what?" she'd asked.

"Escape," I'd said, joking, showing off, having absolutely no idea that it would really happen. "I'll go back to Japan with him, just think"—I'd begun toppling books off my desk onto the floor—"no Thomism! No Courtly Love! No Freud!"

While I was remembering that conversation, I heard, simultaneously, Fuyuko read, "crossing the bridge," in English, and my mother-in-law say, in Japanese, into the receiver, "Crossing the bridge?"

"Is he dead?" my mother-in-law went on. "What hospital? Where?"

Fuyuko stopped reading. Saburo, blinking helplessly, watched his mother.

After she hung up, she slid her hand under her obi and began rubbing her stomach frantically. Her mouth opened and closed, opened and closed again.

"What is it?" Saburo asked.

His mother mumbled, "The shock of it . . . your brother. His car went off the bridge. In this monsoon, he should not have . . ."

"How bad?" Saburo asked.

"It is not known," she said. She seemed to be recovering

her aplomb. I thought I could hear a grim satistaction in her voice, almost as if she was enjoying Saburo's distress, but perhaps I misjudged her.

"We must go to the hospital," Saburo said.

"In this weather?" I wondered, amazed.

"You understand that if he dies, Saburo will be the head of the family," my mother-in-law told me, as if that explained the necessity of driving in dangerous conditions.

"Is our brother going to die?" Fuyuko asked. There were real tears in her eyes, but she was mugging and declaiming like an actress in a Japanese television melodrama. I could tell she was enjoying her histrionics immensely. She had told me she found her oldest brother hard to love; so did Saburo, who put it more strongly.

My mother-in-law started bossing us all around: Find this, pack that. Japanese hospitals don't provide sheets, don't provide food.

"Wouldn't Michiko have brought her own things?" I wondered. (Michiko is my sister-in-law.)

"She might not have had a chance," Saburo explained. "I think she went straight to the hospital as soon as she heard."

"But wouldn't it make more sense to get things from her house?" I wondered. "It's nearer, and it would be his own things, he'd probably rather . . ."

"Get the big jar of *ume-boshi* from the pickle hole," my mother-in-law ordered.

"You'd give *ume-boshi* to someone who was *injured*?" I wondered. (*Ume-boshi* are sour, salty, pickled plums.) "Wouldn't they be awfully hard to digest?"

Saburo dragged me into the kitchen by my wrist. He shoved the kitchen table aside and began prying open the door of the cavity in the floor where the pickles were stored. "How can you be so argumentative," he hissed, "at a time like this?"

"I'm sorry," I told him. "I don't think you should be driving in this weather. It isn't as if there was anything you could do for him, really, and the roads are so dangerous."

"Saburo!" my mother-in-law's voice was raised, shrill. "Help me with the bedding!"

I straggled out to the car, clumsily juggling jars and quilts under an umbrella. I dropped my burdens on the backseat; Fuyuko reached in to rearrange them. I held the umbrella over the lower half of her body. Saburo and his mother had swiveled their heads around to watch this operation. Saburo looked tired and wary. My mother-in-law looked censorious. Some liquid was running down her face, but I couldn't tell whether it was tears or rain.

"So," Saburo said. "Sayonara, Blue Eyes." He rolled up the car window.

Fuyuko slammed the door, stepped back. The car drove off, back wheels churning mud.

"*Itte-rashai*," I muttered. ("Go and come back." That's how you say goodbye to members of your household.)

Fuyuko and I dashed back inside. Despite the umbrella, we were soaked. I left the front door open: The rain was coming down vertically, and I hoped the air would freshen the moldy atmosphere inside. But all that came through the door was the croaking of a million frogs.

I told Fuyuko to go to bed. But after we said good night, and I had undressed and crept into my smelly, unaired futon, she slid open the door of my room and stood there in her nightgown, half visible behind the line of laundry I had hung from the ceiling to dry.

"I can't sleep," she said.

"Try," I told her. "You haven't been trying very long. Read something."

"You know," she said, "if my big brother dies, I think Mother will want Saburo to marry Michiko."

"Fuyu, dear, Saburo is already married." I wanted to sound dignified, but my brain betrayed me. Instead of a standard polite form of "to marry," I used the words a courtier might have used in speaking of the emperor long ago (literally, "Saburo played at marrying me").

I waited for Fuyuko to go into one of the giggling fits my Japanese mistakes usually set off, but I could hear nothing but the croaking of the frogs and the drumming of the rain.

"Even so." She finally sighed.

All I could think to say to Fuyuko was *"Heso magari!"*—an essentially untranslatable idiom that means, literally, "Your navel's on backward," and signifies incorrigible perversity, a kind of helpless, organic violation of the social contract.

I expected her to cheer up, to tell me a monster with no eyes had no right to criticize the location of other people's navels, but she only said, "Good night, then." I heard tears in her voice. Well, her oldest brother was possibly dying and besides, girls of that age love to cry.

The night-light in the hall cast a feeble glimmer into my room. In the near darkness, I kept thinking I saw insects, but the light was too dim to be sure that's what they were. Something large, pale green, and floppy was trapped between the shutter and the window, but was it a moth or only a leaf? Dark shapes seemed to be slithering along the edges of the floor—centipedes? Or mildew forming before my eyes? Something round and brown fell on my face, fragmenting there, but it was not a *geji-geji,* shedding its legs as it landed, only a clump of withered hydrangea dropping from a vase.

I refused to consider the possibility that Saburo's brother wouldn't recover. Instead, I lay there thinking I was going to *get* that mildew. I could iron the back of the sofa, I could train the hair drier on the wall, I could install the sake-warmer in the shoe case.

I wondered whether there could possibly be any truth in what Fuyuko had said. Surely not, I told myself, but it seemed to me that I could remember such situations from Japanese novels. And if Japanese wives could be unceremoniously dumped to keep a brother's widow's money in a family, wouldn't American wives be even more disposable?

Several of the regular *Japan Times* columnists were American women, married to Japanese men. The same issue that had disquieted me with its incomprehensible vocabulary had an article about fellow Americans, married in America to Japanese husbands, who found, in Japan, that they were not entered in the family register, that their children were not legitimate, that they had no rights under Japanese law.

"Like Madama Butterfly in reverse," I mumbled furiously, forgetting for a moment that Saburo wasn't there to calm me down.

I couldn't really believe he would ditch me—and for Michiko, of all people. Why, he didn't even like her. He said she was hard and crass. Still, I couldn't sleep.

Not, I thought, that it would really be a matter of leaving me for Michiko. Not Michiko personally. My rival would be Family, Duty, *Dai-Nippon* ("Grand Old Japan," as my mother-in-law still called it).

And then I felt thoroughly disgusted with myself for taking the possibility seriously enough to waste even a few insomniac minutes on analyzing it. Why should I even half-believe it might happen?

"Why should I believe . . . ?" is such a Western thing to ask oneself. Ten years ago, the night Saburo's brother drove off the bridge, I could still ask myself such questions. It was one of the worst nights of my life.

I didn't sleep at all. I paced through the sour-smelling house, lay down again on my musty futon, got up to pace again. By morning, I had persuaded myself that Saburo had every right to discard me. Hadn't I married him, really, because I realized he'd be a husband who would never— *could* never—invade my privacy (a word that doesn't exist in Japanese)? The conviction that I would never have to declare myself to him, be known by him, that as a foreigner

I would always be so much more generally *other* than particularly myself had seemed like an irresistible loophole in
the terrifying surrender marriage requires.

A doubt of that kind is like mildew. Examine it, and
it seems insubstantial, but if it takes hold, it can do a lot
of damage. When Saburo called in the morning to tell me
his brother's injuries weren't serious, I didn't ask him what
would have happened if his brother had died. I feel that if
I don't admit certain possibilities, I can remain outside
them. I've never asked him. I've never asked anyone.

CONVERSATION
WITH SATELLITES

FOR TERI TOWE

I am smiling (I like to think it is a wry, sophisticated smile) at Morton's barber over the empty place created on my left when Jack's lover is sent off with Morton's camera to document this event. "Why do people photograph parties?" I ask him. "To help the participants remember them? To prove to posterity that we were all really here—together, on this night, in this restaurant?"

The barber shakes his head: He doesn't know, or he doesn't want to speculate. "Are you in show business?" he wants to know. Morton warned me that this young man had theatrical aspirations.

I shake my head. Somehow, we are already disappointed in each other. Nevertheless, he says, "The first time I was in this restaurant, Morton told me he gives this party here for Jack every year when his show is in town, but that's all I know about it. I mean, I don't know who any of these people are. Are they all connected with the show? You seem to know everyone. . . ."

If he wants me to share this knowledge with him, why doesn't he ask me outright?

"The man taking the picture—smile pretty, I think he's got us—is Jack's lover. I can never remember his name. I just call him 'darling,' and no one ever seems to notice, but I don't think you could do that. You only just met him, didn't you?"

Morton's barber nods gravely.

"I think they've been together more than twenty-five years. Isn't that sweet?" I gush, although—or perhaps, at this point, *because*—I can see how my camping embarrasses him.

"Who are those fat people?"

"On Morton's right?" (I ask although there can be no doubt who he means: Ekaterina may not be trim, but compared to that couple, she could almost be seen as svelte.) "They're the Vulgars. Well, that's what we call them, because they are. Their name is actually Bulgar."

"What do they do?"

"Oh, one or the other of them is always president of the Beerbohm Society, that's why they're here."

"Because of *An Evening With Max.*"

"Right . . . Although I suppose Morton has also asked them because they're so appreciative. Morton loves impressing people, you know, particularly *effusive* people." I wonder whether the young man will take to gushing at Morton on the strength of this advice.

"Has Jack ever done anything besides his Max Beerbohm show?"

"No, not that I know of," I inform him.

"Like Hal Holbrook and Mark Twain," the barber compares.

"No, not really," I tell him. "Hal Holbrook *has* done other things, you know." But it seems Morton's barber doesn't know. "We're all supposed to be here as fans of Jack's, of course, but I wonder how many of us are."

"I don't understand—I mean, I think he's fabulous." The young man laughs nervously. "Don't we all think he's fabulous?"

"Mmm—I like him. And his show is very good, but I like it—and him—because I like Max Beerbohm. I suppose Morton 'thinks he's fabulous'—I mean, you know Morton: He loves or he hates, nothing in between."

"What about the other woman, the one on the other side of Jack? Who is she, anyway?" (Not "What does she do?" but "Who is she?"—so unmistakably is she *somebody.*)

"Her first name is Ekaterina; a lot of people call her Katya. No one can pronounce her last name, no one I know, anyway. She's sort of a professional foreigner.

"She used to be an opera singer. I didn't know her then. I've heard her on a couple of records, but I really don't know enough about singing to say how good—or bad—she was. She earned her living, at any rate, and made her way around Europe. Then, when she was about twenty-eight, she got herself entangled with some second-rate cellist who broke her heart. She slit her throat. They rushed her to a hospital, but they couldn't save her larynx."

"You mean she couldn't sing anymore? So what does she do now?" (*Now* he wants to know.)

To my surprise, I feel something that is not so much loyalty to Ekaterina as a notion that I ought not to say disloyal things about her to this somewhat regrettable person. This notion prevents me from identifying her as a fulltime opportunist. Temporizing, I push the silverware surrounding my plate into perfect alignment. All the descriptions for her that come to mind will, I fear, require too much explaining.

"Is she rich?" the simpleminded barber wants to know.

I shrug—urbanely, I hope. "She lives very well; hops all over the world every year. People invite her everywhere.

As for this particular party, she has a special right to be here. She actually *met* Max Beerbohm: She claims he dandled her on his knee one summer in Rapallo when she was a tot."

The young man looks bewildered. It occurs to me that he will soon ask someone what I am doing here. I suspect I have been invited for my facility at making conversation with satellites like himself. That explanation is more bearable than crediting my limited notoriety for my inclusion in this party.

My late lover was a very famous poet. He left me saddled with infuriating debts and a miserable distinction. It is not easy to be identifiable as the subject of one of the best-known poems written in English in this half of the century; a poem that to many people is the last word in disaffection and alienation. It is no easier to have one's penis described in one hateful metaphor, so memorably that as soon as people realize I must be *that* Lewis, their eyes wander helplessly to my crotch. Of all the people seated at this table, the one least likely to have read—or even heard of—"To Lewis" seemed to be Morton's barber, so that I was inclined warmly toward him, although, in general, ignorance has little charm for me.

Jack's lover returns to his place, and the waitress comes back for the third time to see if we are ready with our orders. Although Ekaterina is in full sail on her Mustique story ("And Princess Margaret is in the telephone book, under 'H' for 'Her Royal Highness' "), Jack turns to me to ask what I would recommend. "I have had everything on the menu, and all of it is always excellent," I tell him —truthfully, but not very helpfully.

"I'm having the escargot," his lover declares with cheerful firmness.

Ekaterina is still in Mustique, but it's all very well for her: Her decision has already been made on principle. She invariably orders the most expensive thing on the menu. (My system is not dissimilar. When others are paying, I get the most nutritious thing. But it takes a little longer to identify than the highest figure in the right-hand column.) "I'm going to have the liver persillade," I confess.

"Perhaps the shrimp," Jack mutters dubiously. I notice he's still using his Max Beerbohm voice. It takes time for it to wear off, after a performance; I've noticed it before.

"What, not the steak *au poivre*, burnt to a crisp?" Morton inquires, alluding to a previous collation.

Although no one is even pretending to listen to her, Ekaterina serenely continues her Mustique story while everyone gives their orders.

The barber obviously can't read French, and has undergone an evident transport of relief at the mention of steak. The Vulgars are having *boeuf bourguignon*. As they undoubtedly know, one is served seconds of that dish.

We are all relieved to have discharged the responsibility of ordering, but before the wine question can perplex us, Morton reminds us that we must start with something. Ekaterina laments, "The *coquilles St. Jacques* is really *poetic*, but the shrimp cocktail is always so *succulent*: I just can't make up my mind." I wonder whether she is hoping Morton will urge her to have both.

By the time I have concluded that the soup du jour will yield the biggest nutritional bang for Morton's buck, the barber is in earnest conversation with Jack's lover (". . . my private clients—" says the barber, "Your private clients," Jack's lover clucks after him like a Gilbert and Sullivan chorus, "but by the time I pay my voice coach—" "Yes, of course, the voice coach," "and the dance classes," "But you have to keep dancing!" "And my God! sending out glossies . . .").

Morton is entrancing the Vulgars with an account of someone's antecedents ("grandfather was a blackmailer—oh, yes, it's widely known—in fact, when I interviewed him, he admitted to me—not on the air, of course—that the old man extorted the nomination . . ."). After I've tuned out Morton's dusty scandal, his barber asks me plaintively, "Is she a *good* friend of Morton's?"

Even the not particularly astute mistrust Ekaterina socially. I am at such a loss for an answer he will understand that I pretend to think he is talking about Mrs. Vulgar. "She's the president of the Beerbohm Society," I tell him, turning at once to question Jack (who is scowling at a bowl of vichyssoise) before the barber can request further enlightenment. "I have always wanted to ask you which is your favorite of Beerbohm's works."

"Do you know, for years I would have said *Zuleika* without thinking twice about it, but I've become fonder and fonder of the parodies."

"I have always thought *The Happy Hypocrite* underrated," I murmur.

"Oh, I don't know: It seems to me dated, *really* dated. I would say that most of his work is datable without being *out-of-date*, if you know what I mean."

"I suppose I do." I am trying to think up another question, one which will call forth some of the Beerbohm anecdotes Jack knows—delicious, revealing accounts that did not find their way into either of the biographies. This conversation is what I look forward to about these dinners: It is what makes the other parts of them bearable. I need an inspiration, a quick one, before someone else captures Jack conversationally. My eyes sweep the wall, and I wonder how all these signed photographs come to cover the walls of the restaurant. Do celebrities travel with glossies instead of business cards? Or do they send the photographs the next day? I find myself recognizing, on this wall, Robert Craft. Could it be?

"Why won't that woman shut up?" Jack asks me abruptly. At first I think he means Ekaterina (". . . and of course, at the time, the name Pavarotti didn't mean anything to me, or to anybody, and I said, 'What is the fat *contadino* doing here?' "), but I realize that the woman who owns this restaurant is sitting at a center table and has burst uncharacteristically into song.

"My God! Do you know who that is?" breathes the barber, awestruck, for, now that we come to look at that table, we can see that the restaurateuse is sitting with a *really* high-voltage celebrity, a monologuist who has been making English-speaking audiences laugh for the better part of the century.

Jack's lover leans around the table to ask Morton, "Did I ever tell you I nearly married her dresser, back when I was young and innocent?"

"Young you may have been . . ." Morton tells him gleefully.

I cannot resist informing the barber, "A few weeks ago, I saw Peter Hofmann at that table right there."

"Oh, yeah?" the barber mumbles. It's obvious he has no idea who Peter Hofmann is.

Experimentally, I tell him, "The same night, Christopher Reeve was with a bunch of people back there." I gesture contemptuously toward the men's room.

"You saw Christopher Reeve?" He swallows hard. "Here?" He seems to regard his surroundings with new respect.

". . . whether I ought to say hello?" Jack is wondering. "She doesn't look at all well," he adds happily.

Morton and Ekaterina have started up a game. "Parsleyfal!" he cries.

"Der Fliegender Hollandaise," she contributes.

"Sieg-*fried*?" suggests Mrs. Vulgar, giggling.

"The Noshes of Figaro," I offer.

"Dialogues of the Caramels," Jack puts in.

"Manon L'escargot!" his lover howls.

Ekaterina chuckles. "Rigelato."

"Ossa Nabucco," occurs to me.

"Die Frau Ohne Sauberbraten!" explodes from Morton.

"Un Ballo in Mascara," Mr. Vulgar produces with pathetic pride.

We are embarrassed, except for the barber, who is sulking at his inability to understand the premise of the game. I wonder what the expensive vocal coach teaches him. As if catching my thought, Ekaterina nastily pronounces, "Il Finocchio del West."

"What do you do with ready-made ones, like *Albert Herring*?" I want to know.

The diseuse is sitting with three middle-aged men who look like French intellectuals. Our table is whooping and carrying on like a group of teenaged girls in the proximity of teenaged boys, but no one at that table shows any sign of noticing us, although the restaurant is very small, and half-empty by now. "So Morton will give this party again next year?" his barber asks me.

"Oh, yes," I tell him. But you will not be here. I don't tell him that; it would scarcely be tactful to point out that Morton has a different young man to impress every year —indeed, nearly every time one sees him.

THE FALSE
FALSE PRINCESS

FOR YEVGENIA MARGOLIS

Fairy tales are not about what happened. They're about what happens,
over and over.

There's a princess. She's got to marry a prince, because
that's what princesses do. And she hears about this prince
who's in the market for a wife, so she goes to the castle.

She's not the only one who's heard about the opening:
There's a line going two-thirds of the way around the moat.
And she hasn't been standing there long enough to mop
off her forehead (it's a hot day and she was walking fast)
before three more applicants take their places behind
her.

So she sees that there's a lot of competition. And it's
stiff, too. She's heard that the prince is only interested in
a true princess, and she can see there are a lot of those in
the line. They're easy to spot: They tend not to wear makeup

or nail polish, and when they take their resumes out for a last, nervous glance, our princess can see that these resumes are typed, and not altogether pristine.

There are a lot of false princesses, too. They tend to look a lot better than the true princesses. This depresses our princess, because this prince wouldn't be the first man to drop his standards for a pretty face, now, would he? The false princesses look good-natured, too; altogether easier for a young man to spend the rest of his life with than the true princesses.

Our princess is getting a dim view of her chances, but she doesn't slump (although she feels like slumping), because true princesses don't do that—at least, that's what our princess's nanny always told her. She has developed a routine for keeping herself amused when she's waiting in long lines (banks, post offices, new movies, supermarket checkouts): She recites poems in her mind. She had to memorize lots of them when she was in school, and in those days she never suspected they'd come in handy so often.

The other princesses are beguiling the wait with reading (the false ones are leafing through *People* and *The Star;* the real ones are devouring *The New Criterion* or *Foreign Affairs*) or desultory chatter. Our princess gets through all the Shakespeare sonnets she knows, then starts on the Romantic lyrics, but she gets stuck after "mellow fruitfulness" and by the time she's standing in front of the door marked PERSONNEL, she's saying to herself:

> A bear however hard he tries
> Grows tubby without exercise.
> Our teddy bear is short and fat,
> Which is not to be—

But in the personnel office, there's a lot more waiting around once the resumes (the false princesses have had theirs word-processed and some of them are even on colored paper) are handed in. By the time our princess learns that all of them are going to have to spend the night in the castle before the interviewing starts tomorrow, she's come back to the expense of spirit in a waste of shame.

Rooms are being assigned: doubles. Our princess doesn't know what to hope for. She can't decide whether it would be worse to spend the night listening to a false princess snap her gum or being expected to discuss deconstructionism with a true one.

A true one is what she gets. One who seems relatively human, at that. Our princess had noticed her in the personnel office, putting *The New Yorker* back in her briefcase after looking at the cartoons. Her name turns out to be Anne (but she is not to be confused with the Princess Anne on the cover of *People* magazine).

And it turns out that Anne has insomnia. She turns out the light, and then, just when our princess is starting to feel sleepy, on goes the light again. Our princess watches her roommate leaf three times through *Vogue* in between brief intervals of darkness. After the third leaf-through, Anne catches the opened eye of our princess in the other bed.

"Is the light bothering you?" Anne asks her with meaningless politeness.

"Can't you sleep?" our princess asks Anne.

Anne shakes her neat head, and our princess notices that Anne is wearing a pearl necklace.

"Do you always sleep in that necklace?" our princess asks her, hastily adding, "I mean, maybe it's keeping you awake." She doesn't want Anne to get the idea that she takes any interest in her habits, and besides, it's rude to ask such a personal question so soon after meeting someone, and a true princess avoids nondeliberate rudeness.

Anne nods. "It's good for the pearls," she explains. She sighs. "The thing is, I think there's something wrong with this bed."

"How do you mean, wrong?" our princess asks her.

"There's a lump in the mattress."

"Would a lump in the mattress keep you awake all night?" our princess wonders.

"This one seems to be trying," Anne tells her, crossly.

"Do you want to try trading beds?" our princess offers, with no more graciousness than is appropriate for her rank.

Anne doesn't answer at once. "I wonder—maybe we're supposed to sleep in the beds they assigned to us. I mean, they made a point. Who was to sleep in which bed. Maybe there was some reason. Maybe it's part of some kind of screening procedure, seeing if we can follow directions or something."

"Like the Garden of Eden . . . Do you really think that's likely?" our princess wants to know.

"Well, no, but you never can tell."

So Anne doesn't get a wink of sleep all night, and since she keeps turning the light on and off, neither does our princess. Moreover, ever since Anne said that about the lump in the mattress, our princess has started to feel a lump in her mattress too, although she's sure she wasn't feeling it before Anne said that. Pretty sure, anyway.

The next morning, all the princesses, true and false, are eating breakfast in the dining room. A lot of the false ones are complaining about the food, sending it back. The real ones complain to each other, not to the waiters, and none of them send any of it back. In the line yesterday, the real ones didn't look as pretty as the false ones, and they look even worse this morning. Their unmade-up eyes are blood-shot, and all those within our princess's hearing are talking about the lumps in their mattresses that kept them from sleeping all night.

A waiter is stopping by all the tables. "Hi," he says, "I'm Ken, and our specials this morning—" The real prin-cesses lower their eyes and smile, the false princesses deride him with whooping laughter. "You're a little late! We al-ready ate! Where were *you* last night?"—that's the kind of thing they say to him.

And our princess thinks, "This is the prince. Checking us out in disguise." When the waiter chats long enough to start asking how they like the castle and whether they slept okay, she's sure of it. So when he asks her, she says, "I slept beautifully, thank you."

And he looks quizzically into her bloodshot eyes.

"You did?" he asks her.

"The mattress was so comfortable," she says. All around her, she hears the patrician voices of the real princesses saying things like, "Well, *my* mattress was just like one big bean bag." She knows she's guessed right, and done the right thing.

Sure enough, when she makes it to the final round of interviews, there's the waiter again, but this time he's appearing openly as the prince.

And asking her openly, "Are you a true princess?"

She shrugs deprecatingly. "I'm a false princess," she tells him.

He snorts in consternation. "I'd be willing to swear you were a true princess. I'd stake my life on it. And you passed the pea-in-the-mattress test, but then you lied about it. Why?"

"A real princess wouldn't lie," our princess tells him. "Or so I have always understood."

The prince just keeps staring at her, quizzically. Eventually, she starts feeling sorry for him, or perhaps it's just reflexive class solidarity.

"Unless, of course, good manners forced her to lie. That does happen, sometimes," she remarks.

For a moment, the prince looks happy. Then he looks unhappy again. "That could explain why you lied about sleeping on the mattress with the pea in it. But it doesn't explain why you would lie about being a true princess," he says.

"If I'm a true princess, and I call myself a false princess, then that makes me a *false* false princess, which *is* a kind of false princess, after all, so that I wasn't lying when I called myself a false princess."

The prince says, finally, "I see." After a while, he asks her, "Would you say all those false princesses who say they're true princesses are false true princesses, so *they're* not lying?"

Our princess tells him, "Really, I have no idea." She's not here to discuss her rivals.

Then the prince realizes and says, "Wait a minute! All this brainteaser stuff is beside the point. What I want to know is: *Why* you said it." And he looks at her, challengingly.

With the kind of smile that is an appropriate accompaniment to disarming candor, she tells him, "It occurred to me that anyone who was too sensitive to sleep on a mattress with a pea in it might not be really suitable for royal life. Being so much in the public eye. Besides, I would think a true prince would be sensible enough to know what kind of wife such a woman would make. And it occurred to me that you're really in a very difficult position. You could scarcely tell your personnel department that you wanted an *in*sensitive wife: Someone would be bound to leak it, and the press—"

"But you didn't sleep," the Prince objects stubbornly. "So, by your own admission, you wouldn't be suitable for royal life."

"But it wasn't the mattress!" our princess cries. "It was the princess in the other bed, she kept turning the light on!"

The prince shakes his head. "I like to read in bed," he says, with some regret, for our princess is a pretty girl and he enjoys talking to her. "I'm afraid . . . but would you like to work in our personnel department? You seem to have some insight into my requirements."

So our princess is working in the castle now. They still haven't found a suitable bride for the prince. You might like to apply; I hear they're becoming much more flexible about the qualifications. And they have a terrific benefit package.

PLATONISM

FOR PEGGY REBER

I was delighted to hear that Melody had always treated Paul very badly. Each tale he told gave me a new opportunity of demonstrating my superiority to her, saying wise and sympathetic things in my lovely voice. Let's face it, it's a great comfort for a woman like me, alone in the world and no longer young, to find that a man like Paul—admirable, intelligent, and even handsome—may discover in the end that women like Melody are, after all, not worthy of his attention.

Before their final breakup, Melody had fallen into a state of hysterical peevishness. I was working with Paul at the time; we shared an office. He would tell me about her tantrums, how she dumped the cat's litter box on him at dinner, how she threw the ring he gave her in his face one day in Central Park, how she revealed obscene things about him at a small cocktail party, how there was never any food in the refrigerator but always drugs. Men often confide in me, wanting enlightenment about Women.

I don't remember what advice I gave him. It was a failure, whatever it was, because she finally just kicked him out of their apartment. Just like that, after ten years. Paul had taken me to the opera instead of Melody, because it was *Lulu* and Melody hated Berg. When we came out, a blizzard was raging. He walked me home—we couldn't get a cab—and I asked him whether he'd like a brandy before facing the journey to his apartment all the way across town in the snow. *Lulu* is a long opera; it was late. Paul fell asleep on my sofa, so I put a quilt over him and tried calling Melody. I tried again, several times, but there was never any answer. I figured she was probably stuck somewhere, herself, due to the weather.

By the time Paul got home the next day, she'd changed the locks. Well. Melody wasn't kidding; she never made jokes. If Paul hadn't tried his best to explain, I certainly couldn't blame him. When she let him in to pick up his clothes, some days later, he said she just sat there at the kitchen table eating oysters. He didn't even have the heart to ask for joint custody of the cat.

So for two months he went on sleeping on the sofa in my one-room apartment while he looked for a place of his own. At the same time, we were working together in a cramped little office. Twenty-four hours a day in such nerve-racking proximity condenses intimacy. By the time he found an apartment, we were—in some ways—like a couple married for thirty years.

One day, Paul told me, "I have decided to get you a sapphire. It's the perfect symbol for our understanding." We discussed other things, of course: Logistics, apartments, ceremonies, families, money—those were mere plans. The sapphire, though (his speech about the sapphire), was proof to me that this marriage we had started to think of planning was real to him—real on a level beyond *we will live here, not there; we will have this, not that.* Real as an idea: I'm such a sucker for Platonism, the reality of the Ideal is the only kind I trust. Give me the noumenal over the phenomenal any old day in the week.

"A diamond would be crass," he said, "a ruby would be too passionate, an emerald too indulgent, an aquamarine too cold. A topaz is weak, an opal is sinister." On and on he went, like a Symbolist poet. I still remember every word. "A sapphire," he said, "is just right for us. Modest. Moderate. Cool without being cold. Reasonable. Refreshing, as we are to each other. A relief, like a fountain in a dusty city, like the cool of the evening after the heat of the day."

It was a beautiful speech. How many men do you know who are capable of saying things like that? And if you *do* know any, I'll bet they aren't floating around unattached.

I am no crass materialist. His words were better to me than any jewel could have been. I didn't care that he never bought the ring. For a while, when I was gloomy, I would pause in front of jewelers' windows on purpose to cheer myself up by looking at stones, remembering what he had said. At home, I would take out an imitation sapphire ring I have and squint my eyes out of focus to look at it and pretend.

Paul's speech also quashed a suspicion I had that he'd only started talking about marriage so he could go on staying with me. I mean, could anyone get that eloquent just for a roof over his head, even in Manhattan?

I also thought it proved that he preferred me, after all, to Melody. We spent many happy hours trashing her.

"Isn't it interesting," I said, "that someone so breathtakingly pretty can never manage to be at all beautiful?"

"You must admit," Paul objected, "she has a kind of beauty of surface and texture—"

"Yes, but I think one of the things that's so irritating about Melody is that she's sort of *inanimate*. Shaped like a human being, but with no human being inside," I said.

"She often made me think of a corpse," Paul admitted, "but she certainly has a wonderful complexion."

"Mmm," I agreed. "Like the inside of a conch shell. I always wondered if you put her to your ear, whether you'd hear the roar of the sea."

"Her features and figure are perfect," Paul said wist-fully.

I was afraid he was backsliding.

"Yes, indeed," I conceded, "like something mass-produced."

"I always think of her as something painted by Boucher," Paul told me.

"Right on. The appealing design, the repellent vapid-ity."

"*Talking* to her is exasperating," Paul declared, with a wholeheartedness I welcomed. "Like opening an envelope addressed to you and finding it empty. Over and over," he added.

"Well, she never answers what you say."

"It isn't that she ignores it, exactly," Paul countered.

"No," I conceded, "she hasn't heard it. She speaks on the topic you have raised, without ever responding to your idea."

"Yes," Paul said. "And her voice is *so ugly.*"

"Ironic that she was called Melody," I observed.

Paul nodded. "I got so sick of that voice—so flat, so shrill, so monotonous."

"And that depressing regional accent—where *is* she from? It always makes me think of endless barren plains and harsh weather and subsistence farming."

"It isn't regional," Paul told me, "her sisters don't speak that way at all."

"Maybe it never *changed.* It's pitched like a little girl's."

"But it isn't *fluty* like a child's voice," said Paul. "If she'd been a star of silent films, her career would have been ruined when sound came in."

"How did you stand her? And for ten years?" I asked him, adding, "Says something for your forbearance, I sup-pose."

"Oh, well, I don't know about that," he said. "I mean, at first I—well, I just couldn't keep my hands off her." He stopped. He seemed to be looking at me to see how I would take this, perhaps because he never had any diffi-

culty in keeping his hands off me. But he has often told
me that I have a lovely voice.

"You were young," I said, making my voice go all
indulgent and sympathetic, like an understanding mother's.
Paul looked both sad and defensive. So I told him, soothingly, "Men always love women like Melody, I suppose."

Paul nodded miserably.

"Some radical Freudian might say she was the ultimate
in femininity. . . ."

Paul stared, then grinned, catching on. "An empty
space?"

Finally, Paul did find a place of his own. He never
mentioned the sapphire again, and when the conversation
turned to the subject of marriage one day he said, "My
dear girl, we enjoy each other's company, each other's
conversation. I am cheered, inspired, assuaged by the
knowledge of your existence. But it seems to me that these
are not, really, reasons to marry. Perhaps—one day—when
I'm older and more defeated." And while I felt that those
words were a sad comedown from the speech about the
sapphire, I persuaded myself that his honesty was something to treasure, something rare and hardly won.

"Besides," I told him, sour-grapes-ing, "there is something I don't like about serial monogamy." I, having been
married, had had my chance. And perhaps he had had his
chance too, with Melody Niles.

Some people change jobs a lot; Melody changes fields.
She has yet to find one that interests her. In the course of
her search, opportunities and promotions fall into her lap
like ripe fruit. The strange thing is—and I know this from
people who've worked with her—she isn't really any good
at anything. She's good at succeeding. As such. Not long
after Paul found his apartment, Melody was transferred to
the Paris office of her firm.

Later that year, months after Paul and I had again
discussed—and dismissed—the idea of marrying, we had

a chaste little idyll in Italy. We were spending the final week on the Ligurian Riviera. Apologetically, Paul reminded me of Melody's facility for powerful connections (she has those, rather than friends). He thought it was only right—and I had to admit it might be prudent, at any rate—to let her know where we were.

I was not really prepared for her answering wire. She was going to spend "at least one night" with us, in the dear little hotel we had found in Rapallo. We had gone without reservations, and after checking out everything mentioned in the guidebook, we had stumbled on this delicious place. The garden was hemmed in with rose hedges. Our fellow guests were widows; their median age must have been about seventy. One surviving spouse strutted among them like the Sun King. To each other, Paul and I called him Chanticleer. I often caught him watching Paul with narrowed, resentful eyes.

Paul went to meet Melody at the station. Hoping she would be rumpled and travel-stained, I got out the travel iron I'd ignored since I had packed it back in New York, and was waiting for them posed artfully on a settee in the garden in flawless black linen and a pair of enormous, witty Sphinx earrings I'd found in Rome. I watched them come into the garden. I did not get up. I didn't think I had it in me to sit up so straight. I extended my hand and flared my nostrils, taking in Melody's costume. She was wearing a pale-pink jersey garment that I think is called "rompers." I haven't worn anything like that since I was three.

"How are you, Melody? You look so well. You always do." (Was Paul giving me credit for good sportsmanship? He looked embarrassed.) Gloomily, I noted the splendor of Melody's thighs, peachily tan. I remembered that when advising me on what to pack for Italy, Paul had said that Melody once told him that Italians will ignore any amount of décolletage, but a glimpse of knee will drive them wild. So when I asked her, "How was your trip?" my curiosity was perfectly sincere.

"It took three and a half hours from Rome," she informed us in her toneless voice. I waited to hear whether that was good or bad, but she said nothing more.

"Isn't this place charming?" I asked her, making an elegant, sweeping gesture at the roses and the ceremonious widows.

"No," she said flatly.

"Melody—" Paul bleated.

"I think it's ghastly. You've been here three days?"

I nodded, graciously.

"Aren't you—well, aren't you *bored*? What do you do at night?"

I decided to let Paul answer that one, while I looked particularly blasé, hoping that Melody would think I had something to be blasé about.

He shrugged. "Stroll. Talk. Study Italian," he said, truthfully.

"Is there any place to go dancing here?" Melody wondered.

"We have seen a place . . ." I admitted. "Perhaps Paul would like to take you there after dinner?" I smiled, like someone far too sophisticated to want to go dancing, but prepared to be tolerant of adolescent notions of a good time.

"You eat here?" Melody sneered.

"We got full pensione: It was a bargain," Paul told her. "The food is actually very good. And we can go to the beach after lunch. I mean, if you want to go to the beach."

Melody smiled one of those empty smiles of hers. "I was counting on it. I brought my bathing suit."

I watched her remove from her trendy high-tech bag two little strips of purple Lycra, no bigger than hair ribbons for a doll. No way was I going to watch Paul's eyes watching that all afternoon. I am somewhat older than Melody. I have let my figure go. I wear "fabulous fifties" bathing suits because they show so little of me—and yet, they show too much.

There are situations where I take the foreground and Melody Niles sinks down into the periphery of everyone's attention, becoming something like a Sèvres box on an end table, a lovely little detail in the mise-en-scène. Such situations are few and far between, of course, and the beach is certainly not one of them.

So I asked them whether they wanted to try finding Max Beerbohm's house after lunch instead. Of course, Melody didn't. Of course, Paul could hardly leave her to go with me. So I said that was where I'd be going after lunch.

In the dining room, I watched Melody's table manners in some amazement. I had eaten with her before, yet I had never noticed: She took in her food with an unnerving metronomic regularity. CUT. Chew, chew, chew, chew, chew, chew, swallow. Pause-two-three-four-five-six-seven. CUT. Chew, chew, chew, chew, chew, chew, swallow. Pause-two—it was mesmerizing. Maybe she didn't always do it. It was while I was keeping track of this Stravinskian rhythm that I noticed the ring on her finger.

"Why, Melody," I cried mellifluously (I do a lot of that when she's around, to accentuate the contrast), "that's the most beautiful sapphire I've ever seen!" And I'd looked at many of them, since Paul made that speech.

I noticed that Paul was blushing. "I'm surprised you still have it," he muttered, squirming.

Melody shrugged. "I went back to the park and picked it up. I remembered that poem you wrote when you bought it, and I just had to get it back."

I willed myself to go on eating, drinking, and chatting as though I was not being washed over with rage and desolation, and then found that I was not being washed over with anything of the kind. It was like climbing stairs, step after step till you raise your foot for one more and find that the step you expected isn't there, the flight has ended. A relief. Not like finding a fountain in a dusty city, or the cool of the evening after the heat of the day, but like knowing that what's under your foot—once you get it back down where it belongs—is solid ground.

THE ANGEL OF DEATH

FOR JOHN ODEN

There was a time when Ben, if he found himself back in America, would wind up staying with his former lover, Preston, in San Francisco. Preston, however, has a bad temper and a distressing tendency to become maudlin after his second drink. Besides, Preston lives in the Castro, and after a few weeks the gay ghetto always gets Ben down.

In recent years, Ben has taken to staying with his friend Georgia in New York. Georgia finds anger and sentimentality equally tacky. Ben finds her standards more worthy of rewarding with his presence, and doesn't always bother letting Preston know he's in the country.

He always calls Georgia beforehand, to announce his imminent arrival. Incompetent at calculating time differences, he invariably calls in what is, for her, the middle of the night. In the course of the most recent of these calls, he promised not to impose on her for more than a few days, just until he could find something more suitable.

Since he always makes this speech—yet once found himself staying with her for a full eight months—he knows by now that the assurance is not at all sincere. But long experience has taught him how to deal with Georgia, who has from childhood shown a consistent preference for style over substance.

Although he knows that good manners (hers and his) will suffice to guarantee her hospitality, he takes the additional precaution of placating her with treasures from his travels—Venetian glass, as-yet-untranslated Queneau, this time a Kamakura-bori mirror. Georgia's predictability both bores and comforts him; he knows what will please her.

By now, Ben has developed a conditioned reflex: Whenever, in a plane, he sees the lights of JFK beneath him, he finds himself comparing his career to Georgia's. He has noticed that, approaching New York, he can work up resentment but not envy. Leaving, he finds himself pitying her.

She has been his friend since early childhood. Both of them wanted to be poets when they grew up. And they are. Georgia, from the age of nineteen, has turned out brittle light verse at the rate of two or three poems a year. She has never received a rejection slip, and her work is utterly even in quality.

Ben's own career has been more problematic. He can only publish when he is being clever: No editor has ever liked a poem Ben was proud of himself for having written. He has often been tempted to build a reputation on the strength of his cleverness. He finds himself fleeing this temptation by succumbing to other temptations, in other countries, where he supports himself by teaching English as a foreign language. In New York, he processes the words of others and sponges off Georgia until he has enough money for his next trip.

Why shouldn't he sponge off Georgia? She finds him entertaining, he is a presentable escort, and it is understood that while under her roof he is perpetually on call in that capacity. She pretends to sustain herself by dabbling genteelly in appraisal for Sotheby's, while living in a luxurious, parentally subsidized apartment in Carnegie Hill, surrounded by priceless furniture she was keeping for a sister who married a diplomat. On this visit, however, Ben has been shocked to find the flat denuded: The sister has divorced and reclaimed the antiques.

It is two in the morning, and Ben, who has spent the last fourteen hours in the air, has finally arrived at Georgia's. She has welcomed him with a snifter of cognac, which he is obliged to put on the floor in front of the chintz-covered sofa because there are no tables. Giddy with exhaustion, he finds it hard to cope with this arrangement, harder to concentrate on Georgia's gossip. She has been telling him what's been going on in the city since her last letter.

"Tell me about Doug and Sybil," he demands abruptly, reproaching himself for not having asked sooner.

"Oh, God, Sybil," says Georgia, and shuts up.

"Georgia! Dying? Dead? Tell me."

"Doug is dead, you knew Doug died?"

Ben shakes his head. "Knew he was dying, though—the last thing you wrote was he married Sybil when he found he had AIDS, to be sure that godawful brother wouldn't inherit his money."

"Well, you know Sybil, she nursed him through it like—well, like a wife, a devoted wife. She was practically living at St. Vincent's for five months."

"*Well?*"

"What do you mean by those italics, Ben?"

"I mean, does *she* have AIDS now?"

"Would Doug—I mean to say, how could *anyone*, knowing they were—" Georgia flounders.

"You're being naive," Ben tells her, waspish in the face of mutability. "I never thought other people were very real to Doug at the best of times."

"Umm. Well. No one knows. Believe me, if I don't, no one does."

"Have you asked her?"

"It's not a thing you can just come out and ask someone!"

"You're her best friend, Georgia."

"Well, you're a dear old friend, too. If you think it's so easy, ask her yourself. She's coming over with a statue tomorrow."

"A statue? How's she been able to work if she's been 'practically living' at the hospital?" Ben wonders.

"He died six or seven weeks ago. She cleared out the apartment and moved right back into her studio."

Ben shudders. The thought of Sybil's studio, part of an enormous loft she shares with people he distrusts in a terrifying part of Brooklyn, always makes him shudder. He finds it formidably difficult to face her neighborhood. He has to get drunk to bring himself to do so, even when conveyed to her parties by a numerous and burly escort.

Georgia is going on. "I tried to get her to take some time off for herself, but you know how she is."

"What they call 'self-destructive'?" Ben suggests, attempting condescension to Georgia's superficiality.

"Sometimes I think she's just abandoned, sometimes I think she's sort of saintly. Some of each, I guess. You know how intense she can be. She would *rave*, really *rave*, going on and on about how he'd never see the sun again."

" 'Fear no more the heat o' the sun,' " Ben quotes, glumly. "Not that I suppose Doug had seen the sun since about 1971, given his habits."

Georgia produces a wintry smile.

"Why didn't she stay in Doug's place?" Ben goes on.

"How could she work there? She says this statue's the best thing she's ever done. It's her contribution—I've been asking everyone to help me refurnish the apartment."

"I'll get you a table tomorrow," Ben promises, guilty despite the Kamakura-bori mirror. He gestures to the glasses and ashtray on the floor, nearly upsetting them in his nervous weariness. "This is ridiculous."

* * *

But he winds up waiting for Sybil till she arrives at lunchtime, struggling in from the service elevator with the statue on a dolly. It is an unwieldy thing, swathed in unhygienic old blankets and larger than she is. Like Ben and Georgia, Sybil isn't far from forty, but on her good days she is still very beautiful. This being one of them, Ben, after looking at her, finds Georgia faded and dessicated, and wonders whether he looks that way to her.

Ben tells Sybil he is sorry about Doug.

"But you always despised him, didn't you?" Sybil asks, looking merely puzzled.

He does not know how to respond to her forthrightness. He temporizes with a quizzical stare, finally remarking, "It must have been an ordeal for you, as they say."

"For me?" Sybil is abruptly tearful. "Ben, you won't get AIDS, will you? It's such an awful, awful death."

He assures her dryly, "At the moment I am 'as pure as snow and as chaste as ice'; it seems most unlikely."

To escape her tears, and the distasteful sight of her biting at a stubborn knot in one of the rags binding the grimy blankets, Ben goes to the kitchen and returns with a paring knife.

"No, no, don't cut it!" she cries. "That's a hair ribbon."

Georgia undoes the bindings on the lower half, which is unveiled as Sybil continues her struggle with the knot. Ben sees long black-walnut feet, weight forward; strong legs; an exaggerated erection. Sybil has loosened the knot; she unwinds, exposing a pterodactyl's wing.

"A dark angel?" Ben ventures.

"The Angel of Death," Sybil tells him in a tone of impatient reproach.

Georgia has removed the last covering, and steps back to look. No one says anything for a while. Ben feels tears starting in his eyes. "You know," he says, "you very seldom see a great work of art without knowing in advance that that's what you're going to see." He looks longer. "Except in Italy, of course," he adds.

"You think it's a great work of art? I do, too." Sybil folds her arms and stares approvingly at what she has made.

"I can't believe *I own this*," Georgia says quietly. "It *is* the best thing you've ever done, Sybil, you're right." She turns away, heading for the kitchen. "It's *powerful*, it's disturbing . . . beautiful," she adds without turning back.

"It's horrifying," Ben pronounces, sincerely disturbed. "And beautiful, yes."

Sybil grins at the praise. "I wasn't sure about the wings," she confesses.

Georgia is already back with a bottle, a corkscrew, and three glasses on a tray. Ben picks up the bottle, shaking his head. "Oh, this is all wrong. This is not for this statue; haven't you got something harsh and red?"

Georgia raises her eyebrows, taking the bottle from him and trotting off.

"Does she really think it's beautiful?" Sybil asks Ben. "I promised her a statue, but when I saw where this was going—I mean, *pretty* is more her line."

"True," Ben admits. "But you'd have to be *insensible* not to see what this is. Besides, remember how she loves Goya."

Georgia is back with Chianti. "Blushful enough for you?" she asks Ben, beginning to open it without waiting for his answer. "The head is definitely a head, but I never saw a head that was so much a skull."

"It used to have bushy hair," Sybil confides.

They move to the living room, where Sybil asks Ben to tell her about Japan, which he does until she interrupts him with, "My God! I'm supposed to have been teaching a drawing class for the last fifteen minutes. Could I borrow five dollars? Or would the subway be quicker at this time of day?"

As soon as they are alone with the statue, Georgia tells Ben, "This thing is mine."

"I think you said that before. You're lucky. It's extremely generous of Sybil; it's certainly the best thing she's

ever done. . . . Are you going to keep it here? In the foyer,
I mean?"

"Yes, yes, yes."

" 'Yes, yes, yes'? You *are* excited," Ben observes.

"But not like this," says Georgia. "You realize that's
out of the question."

"What do you mean?"

"Ben, think of the people who come here. The Cad-
walladers. Mrs. Beamish. *Father Knightly.*"

Ben shrugs. "So put it in the bedroom when they
come."

"Ben, it wouldn't be practicable."

"You could put it on casters."

"No," Georgia tells him firmly.

"What do you have in mind, old girl?"

"That"—she gestures at the black-walnut groin—"has
got to go."

"That's the most disgusting suggestion I've ever heard.
And I've heard my share of disgusting suggestions. You
would mutilate a work of art because you might feel some
slight embarrassment about it in front of idiots you don't
respect—"

"And some people I do respect; respect deeply, Ben."

"I'm shocked. I'm simply—shocked."

"Well, get over it, because I want you to help me."

"Help you? In this act of vandalism? This is one of the
most stunning things I've been privileged to see, and you
expect me to help you destroy it for some incomprehensibly
frivolous—"

"It won't be destroyed; it will still be beautiful."

"I don't understand you. I don't care what reasons you
invent, whatever gave you this idea is something so sick I
don't even want to understand it." He is so ashamed of
Georgia that he can scarcely bear to look at her.

"Ben? We've been friends for thirty-five years, do you
realize that?"

"You're drunk, you know."

"So are you. Let's eat," she suggests pacifically.

* * *

They eat bread and cheese and fruit, and they avoid mentioning the statue until Ben can't stand it anymore. "You didn't mean it, did you?"

"You know perfectly well I meant it."

He shakes his head. "I thought I knew you very well."

"I've been thinking," she tells him, "that we'll have to burn it off."

"Burn it off," he repeats blankly.

"Yes. For one thing, it would be a plausible accident. We took the hibachi into the foyer, to look at the statue while we were eating, and some fat caught fire, and—"

"You are mad," Ben tells her.

"Besides," she goes on, "it has to be really artistic damage. I mean, if we just lop it off, Sybil will simply make another one, like, you know that statue of Zeus that's always being vandalized like that? They just keep replacing the . . ."

"Mad," he repeats miserably.

"But we'll have to do it carefully. So it will be beautiful, and Sybil will find it beautiful. You know what a fatalist she is; it will have to be burning."

"I won't let you do this," Ben tells her, surprised by his own vehemence.

"How do you propose to stop me? The thing is *mine*."

"I'm certainly not going to help you."

"Ben, my whole life depends on my friends. And about one-third of them couldn't see this thing the way it is; they wouldn't think the same way about me if they did."

"So roll it into the closet when these limited friends of yours are here."

"This is an extraordinary thing. Do you think it's not going to be talked about, photographed, loaned out eventually?"

"What gives you the right to destroy it?"

"It's mine; Sybil gave it to me."

"You haven't changed since you were six, Georgia. I heard you say that a lot at one time. There's a very nasty side to you, you know, and it always comes out eventually when you don't get what you want."

"Be that as it may, I want you to help me do this, whether you approve or not. You owe me, you know."

"Not that. No one owes anyone that."

"I think I've violated my scruples for you more than once over the years, Ben."

"This is—wanton. I'm going to Sybil. Surely, Georgia, surely you will admit that she has a right to know what you propose to do with what she gave you. Do you think she would have given it to you if she had known?"

"That isn't really relevant."

"Why don't you give it back to Sybil? I'm sure she'll understand. Maybe she'll even bring herself to produce something more *suitable,* something tamer."

"That statue belongs to me. She gave it to me. Besides, I believe I'll be improving it—burning it off is a better symbol for AIDS, if you ask me. And that way, it'll be accessible to more people."

"You *couldn't* make anything like that, could you?" Ben spits. "You would watch a young man die, every minute of every day for half a year, and then you would write something as charming and tasteful and *profoundly* inoffensive as you always do." He stares at her. "Thank you for your hospitality, Georgia, but I find I would rather stay with Preston after all. And I am going to tell Sybil."

" 'I'm going to tell Sybil,' " Georgia simpers. "You haven't changed since we were six, yourself."

At the Art Students League, a languid young man with pink spiked hair tells Ben he just missed Sybil. "Actually, I have to talk to her, do you have a phone number, is there a list?" Ben inquires frantically. "If you don't want to give me her phone number, you could dial it, perhaps?"

"If you've got to talk to her, you'll have to go down there. Claus ripped the phone out of the wall last week."

"To go there? Are you sure? Is there a neighbor I could call?" Ben asks, unnerved, reflecting that the people Sybil lives with are the sort of people who tear phones out of walls on a regular basis. He seems to remember something like this having happened before.

"I wouldn't know," the punk tells Ben.

"No, I don't suppose you would." And Ben, to his own astonishment, finds himself heading downtown in a rancid-smelling filthy taxi. The driver will not consent to wait. "Not around here," he says. "Look, you'll pay me now, I'll come back in fifteen minutes, but if you're not here, I'm gone."

Feeling wily, Ben tells him he has to get the money from someone upstairs, here, and the driver drives off, cursing. Panicking, Ben throws things at the third-floor window, screaming "Sybil! Sybil!" There is no response. He presses buzzers at random; he leans on the row of buzzers. Miraculously, someone buzzes him in.

He steps inside, blinking in the dim light, and is seized from behind. An arm has wrapped him, pinning his arms down, a hand is over his mouth, a black-walnut hand it seems to him in his confusion.

"I just want your money," whispers a voice above his ear. "I don't want to hurt you."

"I haven't got any," Ben screams, "and you are hurting me."

The hands are around his throat; the arms are still pinning his. The man behind him is throttling him. "Help!" Ben screams. "Help! Help!"

As he struggles, Ben finds a curious relief in the concreteness of the thing that is happening to him, and in the fact that he can continue to struggle without puzzling over the rights and wrongs of the situation. But the relief turns into a simple and perfectly pure fear of death as he finds he is losing the fight: His adversary has blocked his windpipe; he can scream no more and he cannot see. His assailant has dragged him down to the floor. Abruptly, he is dropped. His head hits the cold concrete: Sybil's face is very close to his. "Ben, what happened? Ben!" she gasps.

"I was mugged." He finds he is sobbing. "I've never been mugged before; have you ever been mugged, Sybil?"

"Yes, twice, oh, Ben, come upstairs." She is helping him up.

He can't stop crying.

She pours a lot of whiskey into a dirty jelly glass. "Drink up," she urges him, adding, "Claus ran after him; he shouldn't have; I have to call the police."

A large, tragic-looking man walks in.

"He disappeared," the man explains.

"This is Claus, this is Ben." Sybil effects introductions.

Ben is noticing reluctantly how attractive Claus is. He doesn't want to think about it—Claus is a violent man, a destroyer of telephones, a pursuer of muggers, and certainly straight.

"She hit him," Claus explains proudly, "with the chisel. He dropped you, he ran, I ran after. But he is hidden, gone. Have you called police?"

Sybil runs off to a neighbor's apartment to do so. After she comes back, each of them tells the others what happened several times. Just as Ben is on the point of explaining why he came, the police arrive, and the story must be told again. As the cops are leaving, Sybil calls out, "Hey— don't you even want to know what he looked like?" for no one has volunteered that information, and the policemen haven't asked. They don't seem at all interested, except in Preston's address, which is the only one Ben can think to give.

"You're a long way from San Francisco. What were you doing down here?"

"Visiting these people." He getures at Sybil and Claus.

"Oh, yeah," says one of the policemen, who, ugly to begin with, seems to be getting uglier before Ben's eyes. "Well, if there's anything you want to add . . ." He gives Ben a form with some illegible writing on it. "There's the number to call."

When the cops have left, Ben cheers up and tells Sybil,

"I nearly died in the service of art. That's what it boils down to." He is laughing a little hysterically.

When he has explained what Georgia means to do to the statue, and Sybil has clarified it in language it makes him uncomfortable to hear a woman use, she laughs, not hysterically at all.

"I should have known. Really, I should have known. I mean, Georgia. That really wasn't a statue for *her* apartment, was it? I *did* know, remember, Ben, I asked you?"

"You save Ben, I must save your statue," says Claus earnestly. Watching him, Ben thinks Claus must be in love with Sybil.

"No—no. It *is* hers. I gave it to her," Sybil says simply.

"But, Sybil, good God, don't you care?" asks Ben in wondering dismay.

"Actually, no," she tells him, sounding a little surprised by her own admission. "No. I never do, really; once I've made a thing, I tend to lose interest in it. It's the making, really. . . . Don't you feel that way about your poems?"

"No." Ben's mind is reeling.

"Oh, I think we must save it," Claus insists. "It is worth saving, you know. Not like what you make to learn how to make things."

"Well, she isn't going to burn the whole thing. If it's that good, it transcends fig leaves, right?" Sybil appeals to Ben.

"But the whole meaning of it—" he stammers.

"I did give it to her. Let her do what she wants," Sybil tells him firmly, "and you two make up, Ben. You're like a brother and sister."

"She said I was turning into a fussy old pansy," Ben reports.

"Because of that statue?" Sybil wonders.

Ben nods bitterly.

"When all's said and done, it's only a *thing*, after all. I don't mind, why should you?"

"Suppose I find someone to buy that statue?" Claus suggests.

"I don't think Georgia would sell it," Ben tells him slowly. "She has always been able to manage without earning much money; her parents give her so much, you know. And she's so adroit at using her friends." Ben sighs. "She wants to keep it because it *is* beautiful." Sybil's stance makes as little sense to him as Georgia's. "I have never understood women," he tells Sybil, "and just now, if you'll forgive me, I see that as something to be rather proud of."

The pride he mentions sends Ben to Portugal, after six nerve-racking weeks with Preston and Preston's current lover in San Francisco. Portugal is a country where a frugal man can live for a long time on low funds, if he has no wish to be sociable and, no longer believing the straight world wants to hear anything a gay poet has to tell it, has ceased to bother sending out his manuscripts.

PRIVATE LESSON

FOR MICHAEL DENNENY

Mrs. Longo has no aptitude for teaching, and she finds it disagreeable. Mr. Takahashi, whom she is coaching (tête-à-tête) at the moment, seems to her to have no aptitude for learning, and shows every sign of martyrdom.

But no sympathy, no mercy, no affection dilute the rigor of her pedagogical efforts. It is not merely that Mr. Takahashi lacks charm for Mrs. Longo. Her antipathy is grounded in something larger. Mr. Takahashi is a representative of every class of being Mrs. Longo finds herself resenting these days.

1. *He is young.*

"She is young."

"Wrong, Mr. Takahashi, *he* is young. *Read* the sentence, please."

But she *is* young, although she is not as young as Mr.

Takahashi. She is twenty-two; she is five years older than he is. If she were not young, she believes, she would have known better than to make what she now sees as the series of mistakes that have brought her to this classroom where, today, her youth is being wasted on Mr. Takahashi.

He (despite *his* youth) has been studying her language for the past ten years of his life, yet still he uses the feminine pronoun for a masculine antecedent. Why can't he get this he/she stuff straight? In the four and a half months she has known him, Mrs. Longo must have reminded him a thousand times of the necessity of distinguishing between masculine and feminine (not to mention singular and plural). But his imprecision in these matters cannot be attributed to his personal failings, for it is widely shared—not only by all of Mrs. Longo's students at the Dorodarake Special English High School but also by its faculty, who have had far more time, incentive, and opportunity to master the personal pronouns in question.

2. *He is a young man.*

"She is young man."

Mrs. Longo sighs. "Wrong." (She says that often. Her students, including Mr. Takahashi, refer to her behind her back as "Mrs. Wrong-O"—and, since they cannot pronounce the letter "l," that is also what they call her to her face. But they don't know that, since they don't know they can't pronounce the letter "l.") "*He*—not *she*—is young, but, 'He is *a* young man.' "

In being a young man, Mr. Takahashi resembles most of the people who render Mrs. Longo's life oppressive: all the rest of her students, and Mr. Longo, twenty-four, whose fault it is that she is here. On the morning of the day they were married, that young man received an offer from Dorodarake Prefecture—an offer of three teaching positions, to be held simultaneously. As soon as he read the letter, he searched for Dorodarake in an atlas, and discovered it way down at the bottom of the Japanese archipelago, far from any place he'd ever heard of, though he was quite knowledgeable about Japan. He did try calling his fiancée, then, but she was already at the hairdresser's, having orange blossoms stuck in her curls. He had not been able to restrain himself from writing and mailing his acceptance before leaving for the church. He did not tell her what he had done until she had become his wife. "Guess where we're going?" he'd asked her at the altar, with shining eyes.

3. *He is Japanese.*

"She is Japanese."

" '*He* is Japanese,' Mr. Takahashi. We are still talking about the young man. A young man cannot be a 'she.' "

Mrs. Longo has nothing against anyone's being Japanese, of course. But now that she is in Japan, she finds she prefers people to be Japanese on the other side of the world from herself, or at any rate far enough away from her to be unable to thrust uncongenial responsibilities upon her.

"He is *a* Japanese man, but, 'He *is* Japanese,' " Mrs. Longo tells Mr. Takahashi, rashly. As she might have known, this departure from the text has confused him. He does not seem to know what she expects of him now. Her husband, who knows a lot about Japanese culture, has assured her that the whole thing is based on everyone's knowing what is expected of them at all times.

Mrs. Longo's experiences in the Dorodarake Special English High School—where she herself has no choice but to improvise—have tended to confirm this theory of her husband's.

4. *He is a student.*

"She—"

"*He*," Mrs. Longo leaps in hastily.

"She is student."

"She is *a* student."

Mr. Takahashi may be a student, but so what, when he doesn't learn? She is, in fact, no teacher. Doesn't the foregoing prove it? She has just let her student get away with a "she" that should have been a "he." How can what she is doing be called teaching, when none of her students are learning?

She not only hates teaching, but knows nothing about it. The three educational institutions in Dorodarake Prefecture that banded together to import her husband over-assigned his time, scheduling him simultaneously to teach classes in the Dorodarake Special English High School and to hold seminars at Dorodarake University. A meeting was held at which representatives of the three institutions decided that the best way of resolving this schedule conflict was for Mrs. Longo to take the classes at the High School. Her husband told her that, while this decision was reached by consensus, the original suggestion had been Mr. Mutsu's. That is one reason that Mrs. Longo hates Mr. Mutsu, who is the principal of Dorodarake Special English High School, and she suspects it is also one reason why Mr. Mutsu hates her. He had not yet met her when he made that fateful suggestion.

She is *trying* to teach. (" '*He* is *a* student,' " she tells Mr. Takahashi, very firmly.) Her husband is a teacher. He holds a doctorate, and he has taken courses in the teaching of English as a foreign language. He has taught. His students have learned from him. They have made a point of telling him so.

His wife, however, is inexperienced and uncertified. She has nothing to guide her in her endeavors at the Dorodarake Special English High School but her memories of the foreign-language teachers of her own adolescence. She remembers three spinsters who taught Latin in her boarding school as particularly imposing. They were all very tall. And although she never thought to find herself sharing even a single attribute with these sere and celibate classicists—after all, she does. For, although of exactly average height for an American woman, she is, in Japan, gigantic enough to intimidate her students just by standing next to them.

Like everyone else entering the portals of Dorodarake Special English High School, Mrs. Longo sheds her shoes at the door and shuffles around in heelless school slippers that do nothing to augment her height, but she has heard her students sniggering over the drill on comparatives that includes the question "Is she taller than they are?" Although Mr. Takahashi is considered tall for his age, he does not quite come up to her chin, and she towers over Mr. Mutsu by a satisfying foot and a half.

She is trying to acquire other attributes in common with the teachers she remembers as pedagogical beyond all challenge. She is cultivating a donnish sense of humor: "Those who do not know grammar, Mr. Takahashi, are condemned to repeat it." She follows this aphorism—which Mr. Takahashi cannot, of course, be expected to appreciate—with a snorting, melancholy laugh based on an otherwise unmemorable physics teacher's.

Mrs. Longo turns grimly to the blackboard. "MR. MUTSU IS A PRINCIPAL," she writes. "HE IS A PRINCIPAL." Having written these sentences, she enunciates them at Mr. Takahashi with menacing precision. She raises the chalk again.

"MR. TAKAHASHI IS A STUDENT," she writes. "Now, suppose I want to replace Mr. Takahashi with a pronoun." (She smiles—not happily—at the thought of how very much she would like to replace Mr. Takahashi with a pronoun, or, indeed, anything else that might happen to be handy.) She cancels "MR. TAKAHASHI" with a large X, savoring her power. His lips part in alarm. It is the only sign he gives of comprehension.

She stares at him in relentless expectation. Beneath the X, she taps (long, short-short, long) demandingly with her piece of chalk. She has reproduced the rhythm of the song of the cicada (which, as the poet tells us, little intimates how soon it must die). It is also, she notices as she taps, the rhythm of the sentences "He is a fool," and "She is a fraud," and of the phrase "stuck in Japan," and even of the question "Where is my man?" though she cannot account for its presence in her mind, since she knows quite well that her husband is at Dorodarake University, giving a seminar on translation to three ravishing (that is his word for them) graduate students.

Mr. Takahashi appears to have grasped what is required of him. "She is student," he mutters, closing his eyes as though exhausted by this effort.

"*He*, Mr. Takahashi, '*He* is *a* student.' " As she says this, Mrs. Longo writes "HE" under the X, pressing so hard in her exasperation that the chalk breaks. Half of it rolls under Mr. Takahashi's desk. No effort is made to retrieve it.

With the remaining half, Mrs. Longo writes "MRS. LONGO IS A TEACHER." Abruptly, as though to rectify this misstatement, she effaces her name with an egalitarian X. Under this X, she writes "SHE." Inspired, she wags the chalk significantly between the S in "MRS." and the S in "SHE," as if the mystery of yin and yang could be thus laid bare.

Pointing to the appropriate sentences in a parody of patience, she explains. "Mr. Mutsu is a *man*. We must call him 'he.' *You*, Mr. Takahashi, are a man. So we must call you 'he,' too. I"—here she pauses dramatically—"am a *woman*, so—"

Mr. Takahashi looks down, blushing slightly as if embarrassed by his teacher's constant harping on sex. He is, in fact, consulting his watch. Following his eyes, Mrs. Longo sees that their ordeal will be over in four minutes.

The atmosphere in the classroom becomes almost comfortable for a moment. " 'MR. MUTSU IS A PRINCIPAL,' " Mrs. Longo reads encouragingly from the board. " 'HE IS A PRINCIPAL.' 'MR. TAKAHASHI IS A STUDENT.' " To make an inquiring face, she raises her eyebrows.

Mr. Takahashi appears willing to let bygones be bygones. "She is student," he says impassively.

Mrs. Longo points to the words on the board and reads them aloud. " '*HE* IS *A* STUDENT.' Just *read* the words, Mr. Takahashi," she suggests plaintively.

He looks at the words as she points to them again. But he says, again, "She is student," nodding a little self-righteously as he does so.

Is it possible, Mrs. Longo wonders, that all those students and teachers think they are saying "he" when they say "she"? "It is four-thirty, Mr. Takahashi," she points out, although it isn't yet, not quite.

"*Shitsurei sh'imasu,*" her pupil mumbles by way of goodbye, bowing, gathering up his books.

Mrs. Longo begins arranging her own. Her teaching is done for the day, but she is not happy. Other ordeals lie before her.

As abruptly as her arrival in Japan made Mrs. Longo tall, it made her mute and illiterate. When she forgets to ask her husband to translate her shopping list into Japanese, misadventure is inevitable. Once, driven to nihilistic extravagance by her desperation for salad oil and her inability to communicate with an ancient clerk, she went home with the four likeliest-looking containers in the shop. These proved to contain rice vinegar, soy sauce, dishwashing liquid, and shampoo. All of them had, on their labels, pictures of salad vegetables.

She has since learned that salad oil is identified with pictures of kewpie dolls, Betty Boop, or bubbles. Since so many surprising substances are to be found lurking behind Betty Boop and the even more versatile kewpie doll, she sticks to the bubbles. (Cynically, she eschews the cans with *green* bubbles, having concluded that because, in their greenness, they suggest salad, they cannot possibly signify salad. Actually, they do, so she has been unwittingly using frying oil to mix her salad dressings.)

Not that she hasn't made progress in identifying foodstuffs. She knows by now that butter is not to be found in either of the rectangular cardboard boxes with pictures of cows on them, but in a squat cylindrical can with a picture of a snowflake on it (although it is not refrigerated). It's usually out of stock anyway, which she has come to think may be just as well since she has been told that *batakusai* ("reeking of butter") is a viciously insulting way to refer to foreigners, especially Americans.

Mrs. Longo makes a decision. She will find her colleague, Miss Miyagaki, and ask her for help with her shopping list. She does not share Miss Miyagaki's determined friendliness, but she sees no reason not to exploit Miss Miyagaki's ability (apparently unique among the faculty) to understand spoken English, even fairly sophisticated forms of it.

But then Mrs. Longo raises her eyes to the classroom door and spots Mr. Mutsu on the threshold. He enters; she watches and smells his approach. The chalk dust in her nostrils mingles with the sweet fumes of his hair oil. Mrs. Longo is sure that by the time she is free of him, Miss Miyagaki will be gone. So much for her shopping list. (One does not ask one's nemesis for help like that.)

"So, Wrong-o-San, just now you have teached private lesson to Takahashi-Kun, *ne*?"

"You could put it that way," she tells him with determined inscrutability. (Life offers Mrs. Longo few satisfactions these days. Baiting the principal is one of them.)

"So what are you thinking?" Mr. Mutsu asks. Then he makes his question more specific. "Is Takahashi-Kun going to pass the examinations for Tokyo University?"

"Not unless their standards are singularly inexacting," Mrs. Longo informs him, flushing guiltily with the pleasure of spite. She looks forward to his attempts to extract information from her without admitting that he has not understood what she has said.

"Mmmmm," he hums, "Todai standards are very, very . . ."

Mrs. Longo is disappointed in herself. With a little more

effort, she thinks, she could have found a more obscure word than "standards." To penalize herself, she finishes Mr. Mutsu's sentence for him: "High?"

"Exactly so," the principal confirms.

Now it is Mrs. Longo's move again. "How regrettable for Mr. Takahashi," she ventures.

Behind his thick lenses, Mr. Mutsu blinks. "If he can become a doctor, it will make his mother happy," says Mr. Mutsu.

"No doubt," Mrs. Longo tells him, her perverse elation augmented by a grudging admiration of Mr. Mutsu's skill at this game, "but his astonishing incompetence is liable to blight his medical career."

"I am glad to hear you say that," Mr. Mutsu informs her.

She cannot enjoy her victory. Not only were there no spectators, but it was too easy. She would have preferred a longer volley. Perhaps she will have to make new rules for herself: no taking advantage, say, of the confusion between "r" and "l."

"Why?" she inquires, but without real relish. "Don't you like his mother?"

"Mrs. Takahashi has plenty of money," Mr. Mutsu remarks.

Mrs. Longo knows all about Mrs. Takahashi's fortune. It came to her from her father, a plastic surgeon whose curious specialty was the restoration of ruptured hymens. (Miss Miyagaki has explained to Mrs. Longo that the old doctor's skill had been in great demand in the postwar decade.) Mrs. Takahashi evidently believes that her only son is most likely to replicate his father's prosperity by imitating his academic career, and to this end she has had him educated, coached, and tutored unrelentingly.

Mr. Mutsu resumes caution. It appears to Mrs. Longo that he is even now unaware of his defeat, but he seems to suspect that something is amiss. "When her son has acceptance from Tokyo University, Mrs. Takahashi will give us a language lab."

Mrs. Longo finds she has no appetite for a second round. "Mr. Mutsu," she says, "Tokyo's entrance exams are the most difficult in this country, aren't they?"

Mr. Mutsu throws back his small, fragrant head and opens his mouth very wide. Mrs. Longo does not know whether he is overcome by relief at having understood every single word of one of her sentences or whether he is dramatizing his inability to express the surpassing difficulty of Tokyo University's entrance exams.

She looks away, rejecting intimacy with Mr. Mutsu's bridgework. She goes on. "Mr. Takahashi is the worst student I have." As a kind of mocking consolation for the disappointment she must just have occasioned him, she decides to present Mr. Mutsu with an example of what he morbidly calls "living English." "He doesn't have a snowball's chance in hell."

"How can this be?" Mr. Mutsu asks. He looks surprised, which surprises Mrs. Longo.

Mr. Mutsu has informed Mrs. Longo on previous occasions that he is on record (in an article in *The Journal of Southern Japanese Educators*) as having great respect for the analytical capacities of the Western mind. He seems to listen passionately as Mrs. Longo itemizes: "He is stupid. He doesn't study. He doesn't learn. He doesn't seem to know how." (But as she says these things, her mind provides a counterpoint: She is stupid. She doesn't teach. She doesn't seem to know how.)

"He *only* studies," Mr. Mutsu protests. "He don't do nothing else. Every day after school she goes to English classes in *juku*, she comes home at nine o'clock in the night, then there is a private tutor coming to his house. And every weekend it is the same thing."

Mrs. Longo sees that the distinction between learning and being taught is as meaningless to Mr. Mutsu as that between "he" and "she." And yet Mrs. Longo knows for a fact that this man holds two doctorates, one in Education and one in English Literature. He boasts, moreover, of having spent a semester at Southern Methodist University.

"So when does Mr. Takahashi do his homework?" she asks.

"In the night, with that private tutor." Mr. Mutsu glares at Mrs. Longo, as though she should have figured that out for herself.

She sighs. She thinks, So Mr. Takahashi has never been left alone, unchaperoned, with a piece of information. No wonder he doesn't learn. But she does not say these things.

"Mrs. Longo," Mr. Mutsu says, "if Mr. Takahashi does not pass the entrance examination for Tokyo, there might be some serious consequences."

"Maybe someone else will give you a language lab," Mrs. Longo says, hoisting her shoulder bag. But conversations with Mr. Mutsu are not so easily ended.

"The rate of suicide among children in Japan is the very highest in the world, isn't it so?" he persists.

Mrs. Longo has heard Mr. Mutsu boast about many of the global superlatives Japan has established, from the smallest average bust measurement to the greatest per-capita distribution of both eyeglasses and violins, but it seems to her that he is really scraping the bottom of the barrel of preeminence now. Then she sees why he has dragged out this statistic, and is annoyed. "Mr. Takahashi isn't about to kill himself," she asserts, wondering as she does so why she is saying it—Mr. Takahashi's character is utterly opaque to her. (Although she made the statement with confidence, she finds she is afraid.)

The principal hastens to document his assertion. He extracts a newspaper clipping from his pocket. "Twelve years old," he says, although the clipping looks quite recent. Since the story is in Japanese, Mrs. Longo cannot read it. Instead, she stares at the photograph that illustrates it, and decides Mr. Mutsu is referring to this girl. "She does look a little bit like Mr. Takahashi," she observes. "Heavyset."

"Using gas. Thirty-two persons in that building also died because of that explosion. She wrote a letter to say that she killed herself because she was ashamed to the spirits of her ancestors since she failed the examination for middle school."

Mrs. Longo cannot imagine Mr. Takahashi doing anything newsworthy, even to assuage the presumably implacable spirit of the renovator of maidenheads. "I have done my best with him," she assures Mr. Mutsu dryly.

"Ah, so?" Exuding these syllables, the principal puts the clipping back in his pocket. "Maybe if he don't pass the examination this year, next year he will try again. 'If at first you don't succeed, try, try, try again.' "

Mrs. Longo is afraid he will go on to identify this saying as "living English," but he does not. Instead, he says, "So maybe next year you can do a private lesson to Mr. Takahashi for three hours every day."

Mrs. Longo feels the floor of the classroom shaking beneath her feet. She grips the edge of the desk, which trembles, eluding her grasp. She attributes these phenomena to her extreme dismay at the possibility Mr. Mutsu has just mentioned until, observing the framed face of the Minister of Education lurching away from the map of the world on the wall, she realizes that an earthquake is taking place.

Proust-like, Mrs. Longo is invaded by memory: The sensations of a terrible undergraduate party repossess her. The punch, which she remembers as smelling something like Mr. Mutsu's hair oil, was harsh and even looked garish, but she could not stop drinking it, because the young man who would be but was not yet her husband would not stop dancing with a smug and inexplicably popular anthropology major called Mary Jane Becker. Then, as now, the room and its furnishings wavered and shifted around her: With painful intensity, she remembers how much she wanted him to take her home. She glares accusingly at Mr. Mutsu. (*Mr. Mutsu is a man.*)

"That was a small, everyday kind of earthquake," he informs her. He looks up at her, a nervous laugh escapes him. "Take no notice, dear lady."

"I will not be here next year," she hears herself saying.

"Maybe so," Mr. Mutsu concedes.

"My husband's contract is for one year," she hears herself saying.

"Maybe Dorodarake will renew that contract," the principal speculates, adding, "Do we say 'to renew'?" Mrs. Longo takes no notice. Tears start to her eyes. Her husband would not do that to her, he couldn't. But look what he has already done.

Dainty little Miss Miyagaki glides by the door of the classroom, her pale gauze sleeves flapping like the wings of a good fairy. Mrs. Longo's shopping list, at least, is not a lost cause after all. "Excuse me, Mr. Mutsu, I must speak to Miss Miyagaki."

Mrs. Longo does not particularly want to share a soggy and chemical éclair in the café called Moscow in the neighboring town of Shizunde (an overgrown fishing village, really), but there is no place to go for a snack near the high school. Besides, for some reason Miss Miyagaki seems extremely eager for the excursion, and since it will probably result in Miss Miyagaki's actually doing Mrs. Longo's shopping for her, Mrs. Longo agrees to go. The bus to Shizunde is filled with the gloomy uniforms of Dorodarake Special English High School, so it is not until the two women are seated on the squat but spindly imitation brass café chairs, picking delicately at the ersatz éclair, that Mrs. Longo feels free to tell Miss Miyagaki, "Mr. Mutsu is such a *creep!*"

"But he perseveres," Miss Miyagaki says mildly.

Mrs. Longo looks at her blankly. "Are you sure that's what you mean to say?" she asks at last.

Miss Miyagaki, blushing, removes an aging dictionary —twice as thick as her delicate wrist—from her bag. "*Ganbaru*," she reads, "to persevere, to keep at it, to continue."

"I wish he wouldn't," Mrs. Longo tells her.

Miss Miyagaki giggles delightedly. She is happily conscious of the interest her exotic companion evokes in the other women in the pâtisserie. She masticates her mouthful ostentatiously, to let Mrs. Longo know how much she is enjoying this cosmopolitan occasion.

Mrs. Longo winces at the consequent sights and sounds. A cultural abyss seems to gape between her and her colleague. She knows that Miss Miyagaki is regarded as a model of deportment, but Mrs. Longo will never, never, never get used to Japanese table manners. Somehow in a person of Miss Miyagaki's delicacy, refinement, and intelligence, they are all the more distressing.

Mrs. Longo does not know why Miss Miyagaki is laughing, since what she just said about Mr. Mutsu was not intended as a joke. She needs to vent her indignation. She tries again. "You know what he was telling me, in the classroom just now when you walked by?"

"I did not hear him, tell it to me, please, I would be delighted," Miss Miyagaki requests carefully, unfortunately deciding to augment the encouraging politeness of her words by sipping her tea very loudly. "And then I will tell you something, too."

"He told me that if that Takahashi idiot doesn't pass the Tokyo entrance exams, next year I might—" In midsentence, Mrs. Longo realizes that she cannot very well go on as she is about to. How can she tell Miss Miyagaki (*She is Japanese. She is a teacher*) how homesick she is, how much she hates teaching, how awful the prospect of another year here is to her? Never mind: She has no shortage of grounds for denouncing Mr. Mutsu. "He told me he might kill himself. And he sort of implied that if he did, it would be my fault."

"*Hora!*" Miss Miyagaki exclaims. "Maybe you should stop teasing him."

"*Teasing him?*" Mrs. Longo is sure that in all her dealings with Mr. Takahashi she has shown the patience of a particularly forbearing saint. "Get out that dictionary again."

Miss Miyagaki, her tiny hand trembling under the weight of the heavy book, looks up the word and reads, frowning, "Tease, make mock of, make fun of."

"I have never *teased* Mr. Takahashi," Mrs. Longo says, trying to straighten her back without engulfing her head in the vermilion Plexiglas shade of the low-hanging lighting fixture.

"Not Mr. Takahashi, Mr. Mutsu," Miss Miyagaki explains, hoping that this confusion has not arisen because she expressed herself incorrectly. She looks a little put-upon. Her enthusiasm for the English language is great but not boundless.

Mrs. Longo attempts to restore some semblance of communication to their conversation. "Mr. *Mutsu*? Why would Mr. Mutsu kill himself because Mr. Takahashi flunked an exam?"

"Of course," Miss Miyagaki amplifies, "he would not really kill himself because Mr. Takahashi did not pass that examination; he would really kill himself because you have been teasing him and he has lost face very much when you teased him. But if he explains that that is *why* he is killing himself, then he will lose still more face. So he needs some excuse for killing himself, and if Mr. Takahashi fails that examination, he will have that excuse. People will say it is a very noble—a very elegant?—reason for suicide." Miss Miyagaki is a little breathless after all these complex English sentences. She hopes she has made herself clear.

Mrs. Longo is quite overwhelmed. She has come to trust Miss Miyagaki's assessments of things. And Miss Miyagaki's predictions—even when they are extremely improbable, like the one about the shortage of toilet paper and the fact that several consumers would be trampled to death when it reappeared in supermarkets—have always come true. So it seems it is actually possible that the game she has improvised for her private amusement could drive a man to suicide.

She hates Mr. Mutsu, but not with that kind of hatred. She certainly doesn't want to compass his death. "Do you really think he would?" she asks frantically.

"Maybe so."

"And you're saying I would be responsible?"

"Don't worry," Miss Miyagaki murmurs. "I will tell no one. I think"—here she lowers her bright eyes modestly, perhaps to disavow the inherent boastfulness of her assertion—"I am the only one who can see that you talk on purpose so he won't understand." Raising her eyes again, she sees the distress in Mrs. Longo's. "I will tell no one," she repeats.

Dizzying sequences of lethal causality unfurl in Mrs. Longo's imagination. If it is possible—as it seems to be—that Miss Miyagaki is right about Mr. Mutsu's putative suicide, then is it also possible that Mr. Mutsu is right about Mr. Takahashi's?

She seeks clarification. "Are you saying that Mr. Mutsu might kill himself—because I've humiliated him—if Mr. Takahashi just flunks, or will Mr. Takahashi have to kill himself?"

"Don't worry," Miss Miyagaki insists soothingly. "This will not happen."

"Didn't you just say it might?"

"But Mr. Takahashi will pass the examination, so Mr. Mutsu won't have that excuse for killing himself. Nevertheless, I think maybe you should stop teasing him—if you don't want him to kill himself—because some other excuse might happen. You don't eat this éclair?"

Mrs. Longo stares reproachfully at Miss Miyagaki. "But Mr. Takahashi *can't* pass that examination. Not the English part. Believe me—I know, I teach him every day."

"But I am his teacher too," Miss Miyagaki protests. "Advanced English Grammar. And English Reading Comprehension. I know that he will pass. Mr. Takahashi has many advantages. In our school he has many, many more hours of English classes than students in some ordinary high school. And he has still more in *juku* after school. He has a tutor, too, I mean more than you, yet another one."

"Mr. Mutsu told me. Given all that, he's really amazingly bad at English."

"No, no, he is not so bad. I know very well about Mr. Takahashi, I was giving him private lessons too, at one time. Poor Mr. Takahashi. He seems to be more stupid than he is, because he is often falling asleep. I was going to his house from eight o'clock to ten-thirty at night. He was sleeping sometimes with his eyes open, saying crazy words from his dreams. I was asking him about maybe the gerund and the predicate adjective, and he was all at once yelling something about spiders. This happened four years ago, he was a little boy. I felt so sorry for him, I could not awaken him. One time his mother came in and saw that he was sleeping, and she poured a glass of water on his head. And then she told Mr. Mutsu to find another tutor, because I was a thief, to take her money and let her son sleep.

"But he can pass that exam, I am sure. You see, you have no way of knowing about that because you do not speak Japanese."

"The English exam is in *Japanese*?" Mrs. Longo asks limply.

"Of course there are some examples in English . . . I am not sure if he will pass this year. If not, he can next year, for sure. Poor Mr. Mutsu, then."

Mrs. Longo's mind, wearied by Miss Miyagaki's revelations, pains her. Her long American legs hurt too, cramped by the diminutive furniture. "If you think Mr. Takahashi is going to pass this exam, why do you say 'poor Mr. Mutsu'?"

"Oh." Miss Miyagaki, enjoying the éclair, is expansive. "Then Mrs. Takahashi will give Mr. Mutsu a language lab. *Imagine* that. In some big room, there will be maybe one hundred tape recorders with foreigners' voices talking all day, and Mr. Mutsu will understand very little. For Mr. Mutsu, it will be as if one hundred of Mrs. Longo were teasing him forever. That is why I say 'Poor Mr. Mutsu.' Especially now that Mr. Mutsu has helped—"

Miserably, Mrs. Longo interrupts her colleague. "If that happens, it won't be my fault."

Miss Miyagaki follows her reasoning. "You have not been teaching Mr. Takahashi to pass exams," she agrees.

"I have taught him *nothing*." Mrs. Longo snorts.

"That is all right," Miss Miyagaki soothes. "You are not supposed to teach him nothing. No one expects you to. Really."

"Then what am I supposed to be doing with all those students, if I'm not expected to teach them anything?"

Miss Miyagaki finds this question difficult, but she is no coward. She flattens the paper doily in front of her with the tines of her gold plastic fork. "In a way, of course, there is no point in having a native speaker to teach these children. They are not ready to learn English from a native speaker. But in another way, it is good. It is most important for them to see that you are human beings, too. We don't have foreigners in Dorodarake Prefecture. So we only see how foreigners look in pictures or movies—like big hairy barbarians, you know? How can we see how foreigners are people just like us Japanese, after all, strange eyes and strange customs nevertheless?" As she speaks, Miss Miyagaki hears herself making mistakes, but they do not distress her. She glows with the awareness that what she is expressing, however awkwardly, is beautiful. "So I am so happy you are here." Tears come into her eyes, she is so moved by what she has just said.

Mrs. Longo nods. "But I'm not expected to teach them any *English*?"

"You teach them English, a little bit—maybe some idioms?—but even if they don't learn in your class, it is not really wasting their time."

"*Their* time?" Mrs. Longo growls.

Miss Miyagaki is startled by her tone. Her glow vanishes abruptly. What was wrong with the sentence she just uttered? "*Her* time?" she guesses wildly, but even as this preposterous emendation flies from her mouth, she realizes that she had used the pronoun correctly. But what else is Mrs. Longo growling at? She is sure she can say "waste time"; it occurs in an example sentence she uses frequently in drills. "Time . . ." she falters, then is inspired to squint at her watch. She jumps to her feet; her sleeves flutter ethereally. "Mrs. Longo, we are now missing the last bus!"

The two women dash, panting, through the maze of Shizunde's shopping arcade. Miss Miyagaki bangs on the bus's closing doors, and breathlessly urges the driver to open them for the foreigner who is staggering toward his vehicle. Clutching her side, she smiles, seeing this gesture reproduced on a larger scale by Mrs. Longo, as though in a magnifying mirror. The truth of the assertion she has just made about their common humanity seems vividly exemplified.

By the time the bus deposits them in front of Dorodarake Special English High School, the shops nearby (such as they are) will be shut. "Oh, Miss Miyagaki, what will I do? I was hoping you could help me with my shopping; I have nothing to give my husband for dinner." Mrs. Longo gasps, sinking onto a jouncing seat.

Miss Miyagaki's delicate hand rummages in her bag, extracts a parcel. "Please take this. It is excellent, very fresh, I bought it today."

"Oh, I couldn't possibly—"

"Oh, you must have something for Professor Longo to eat for dinner! I have another thing to give to my mother. You take that, please."

Mrs. Longo peeks into the parcel. She sees purple tentacles pimpled with grayish-white suckers. She does not, and she doubts that her husband will, eat octopus—especially since she has no idea of how to cook it. "It's very kind of you, Miss Miyagaki, but—"

Miss Miyagaki will not let Mrs. Longo refuse her gift. Beaming, she slips it into Mrs. Longo's bag. "Now you have everything you need!"

Mrs. Longo is at a loss for words.

Miss Miyagaki takes advantage of this unusual condition. "Mr. Mutsu is a big fool, everybody knows that," Miss Miyagaki remarks abruptly, "but he is a kind man. He is arranging a marriage for me. I am very grateful, because my mother is poor and cannot do it. And I cannot be unmarried any longer." She peers shyly up into Mrs. Longo's face. "We don't do that in Japan. We must be married. I think it is very different in America." She giggles. "I will learn about America, if I marry this man Mr. Mutsu has found for me. He lives in Kitakyushu now, but next year he will go to teach Japanese children in New York, and if I marry him, I must go with him. It is not yet arranged; I have not yet met this man, but I want to tell you about it now, because if that happens, I will be just like you, then, isn't it so?"

Mrs. Longo notices that her mouth is open, and shuts it. Then she opens it again, but all that comes out of it is "Oh, Miss Miyagaki—"

"I have never visited any foreign country. Or any very big city, even in Japan," Miss Miyagaki tells her. "Do you think I will like to live in New York?"

Mrs. Longo remembers the words she so thoughtlessly threw at Mr. Mutsu: "a snowball's chance in hell." Because although Mrs. Longo thinks of New York often and with intense longing, now, trying to imagine Miss Miyagaki living there, she can think only of its squalor, its cruelty, its ever-present possibilities of violence. "This man you would be marrying—?" she hears herself ask.

"I do not have his photograph here. In some way, I think I know him, although I have not met him. He is a teacher of English, too; he has written some books that we use in school." Miss Miyagaki pulls an English text from her bag.

Mrs. Longo knows it well; it has brightened many a bad day for her. At the end of every chapter, in dialogues called "Sample Conversations," characters with names like Mr. Brown and Miss Johnson greet each other with sentences like "Excuse me, you look familiar. Didn't I meet you in the bathtub last night?"

Miss Miyagaki will be facing New York with no one to help her but the author of these dialogues. "Oh, Miss Miyagaki . . ." Mrs. Longo hears herself trail off again, for what can she possibly say? But something is certainly called for: Though the gesture doesn't seem adequate, she lunges gently down, intending to plant a sisterly kiss on her colleague's cheek.

The bus veers sharply, and the kiss lands instead on Miss Miyagaki's mouth, with much more force than Mrs. Longo had intended. Drawing back, she is horrified at the expression (like an international graphic for shocked disgust) that is disfiguring Miss Miyagaki's dainty features as she wipes her mouth reflexively with the edge of a fluttering sleeve.

"I'm sorry, I didn't mean . . ." Mrs. Longo scans Miss Miyagaki's face anxiously for signs of returning self-possession.

"You mean something good, I know," Miss Miyagaki assures her eventually, in an unsteady voice. "But we never do that in Japan."

Bouncing helplessly on the seat of the lurching bus, crushing her shrinking colleague against the window, wondering what she is going to do about dinner, Mrs. Longo watches Miss Miyagaki's eyes taking a shamed, furtive survey of the fellow passengers who have observed this disgrace. They begin standing up; so does Miss Miyagaki. Mrs. Longo rises too, and is aware, as usual, of being much taller than anyone around her. Nevertheless, and for the first time in this country, she feels extremely small.